AN INCONVENIENT ARRANGEMENT

ROSE ROOM ROGUES ~ BOOK THREE

CALLIE HUTTON

r

London, England
May, 1892

*D*ante Rose, by-blow son of the late Earl of Huntington, brother to the current earl, Hunt, and older brother Driscoll, all partners in the exclusive Rose Room gaming club, stared at the missive in his hand. Another summons from their mysterious contact at the Home Office.

He had warned his brother, Driscoll in his terse manner earlier in the week that the assignment was coming. He flicked the paper with his finger and left the office to seek Driscoll, most likely in the breakfast room besottedly staring at his wife, Amelia. Both brothers had succumbed to the wiles of women in the past two years and had taken the march down the aisle to cut off all the fun and freedom a man found in life.

Not him. Never him. He had no title and as a by-blow of his father didn't stand in line for the title no matter what happened to Hunt and Driscoll. Let his brothers wrangle with the restrictions of marriage and produce nurseries full of offspring. He would live his life the way he wanted until he took his last breath.

And that did not include tying himself to one woman. He liked women too much and despite his reputation, he believed in adhering to one's marriage vows. He refused to believe that had anything to do with his birth status since he'd always been treated the same as his brothers.

Same nursery, same schools, same opportunities. Unsurprisingly, his step-mother did not shower the love on him as she did his brothers, but she always treated him with respect and his father's attention and encouragement had more than made up for it.

He groaned as he entered the dining room. "Oh, damn, brother. Can't you two keep your nonsense confined to your own bedroom? Or at least your own house?" Dante shook his head at his brother and sister-in-law just breaking apart from a kiss.

"Well, aren't we in a fine mood this afternoon," Driscoll said as he picked up his coffee cup.

Dante poured a cup of coffee and filled a plate with eggs, toast, tomatoes, and sausage. Although it was breakfast, due to the hours they worked at the club, the meal was served well past noon in the private dining room on the second floor of the establishment.

He placed his food on the table and leaned his forearms on either side of the plate and looked Driscoll in the eye. "My day is fine, but your day is about to become more difficult, brother."

Driscoll raised his brows. "Why?"

Dante shook out his napkin and placed it on his lap. "The summons from the Home Office I told you about has arrived. As usual, our friend said nothing in the missive except that it might take *some time.*"

He remembered the conversation between him and Driscoll

in the office earlier in the week.

"I will be gone for a while."

"Home Office?" Driscoll asked.

"Yes."

"How long?"

"Not sure."

"When?"

"Soon."

"We'll handle everything."

"Damn." Driscoll ran his palm down his face. "Hunt might be able to help out a bit, but with another baby on the way, he's a bit—distracted—shall we say?"

Dante waved his hand. "The man has a household full of help. Plus, his wife, who spends all her time hanging over her child's bed making sure he continues to breathe. One would think she'd moved past that by now."

He took a swallow of coffee. "What about Keniel? I thought we planned to have him work extra hours. He's always ready to help out."

"He asked for a few days off since he's close to buying a townhouse."

Dante shrugged. "I'll send a note and tell him he needs to be available now and take time here and there to settle himself. He knew his hours would be flexible."

"Good morning, Dante," Amelia said with a slight grin.

"Oh, sorry." He offered her his famous slow smile that had the ladies ready to drop their undergarments. Unfortunately, or perhaps for Driscoll's sake it was fortunate, Dante had no effect on Amelia. He dipped his head. "Good morning, sister."

She looked at Driscoll. "I can continue with dealing at my old table as well as help with the books. That would free up Dexter to assist with the management."

Driscoll shook his head. "No. You are seven months pregnant. I'm not even happy with you coming here to do the books."

"Oh for goodness sake, Driscoll. I dealt for months before we married. It never bothered you before."

"Incorrect, wife. It bothered me a great deal, but I had no control over it. Now I do."

Dante laughed. *Shite*, the man was stepping right into it.

Amelia sat back and viewed her husband with steely eyes. "Excuse me?" she said, her eyes boring into her husband. "Are you suggesting you have control over me?"

Dante shook his head as he shoveled the food into his mouth. Another reason to not get involved with a wife. They never stayed where you put them, never did what you told them, and when things didn't go their way, they cried. Or threw things at your head.

"Now, sweeting, you know that's not what I meant."

Amelia crossed her arms over her chest. Dante swore he could hear her foot tapping under the table. "What exactly was it you meant, then, *sweeting*?"

Taking the last gulp of coffee, Dante stood. "I shall leave you two lovers to work out this little issue. I have a few things to finish this afternoon before I meet with Sir Phillip DuBois-Gifford."

Although that was the name their contact used, the brothers were quite certain it was not his real one. Furthermore, their meetings with the man took place in a small, somewhat shabby townhouse in a lower-class neighborhood. Dante was certain that nowhere in the Home Office records was there a Sir Phillip DuBois-Gifford.

He returned to the office they all shared and pulled out the few files in which he had matters to finish. He scribbled off a quick note to Hunt, advising him of the new assignment and that he needed to spend a bit more time at the club. Who knew, maybe by now his oldest brother was ready for more than nanny-sitting.

He pulled out the information on Mr. Keniel Singh. The man had appeared at the club one day asking for a job. Despite his young age, he had an impressive background, having managed a large plantation in Jamaica for several years. Counting back, that meant he'd taken over the plantation when he was only nineteen.

What resolved the question of hiring him was the fact that the plantation he'd managed had belonged to the brothers' father at one time but had been sold a few years before, upon his death.

He closed the file with Keniel's information and left it on Driscoll's desk. It took him about an hour to finish up and then he was off to meet with Sir Phillip. He made his way to the gaming floor and gave the two missives he wrote to one of the security men and asked that they be dispatched immediately. Neither Driscoll nor Amelia were in sight—most likely in the bedroom upstairs making up for their argument—so Dante left the club, not knowing when he would return.

Sir Phillip was always vague about how long assignments would take.

Thinking it would be best to not yet pack for whatever it was the man had in mind, Dante took the club's carriage to Sir Phillip's townhouse.

He bounded up the steps and dropped the knocker only once before the middle-aged housekeeper opened the door. "Good afternoon, Mr. Rose. Sir Phillip is in his study."

"Thank you." Dante made his way up the stairs and down the corridor to the overcrowded office that symbolized Sir Phillip.

"Come in, come in, Dante. So nice to see you. It's been a while since I had something that's perfect for you."

Dante took the seat across from Sir Phillip. "What is it this time? You're correct it has been a while."

Never one for small talk, Sir Phillip leaned forward and delved right into the matter. "There is spying going on at the German Embassy. While that generally happens in a small way, this is more serious because whoever is passing the information along is privy to things the Home Office is deeply concerned about. Needless to say, we are not happy about that, and we want to confirm first of all that this is true and if the person we believe is involved in this is who we suspect. We will then make arrangements to stop it."

Dante had no desire to know how they intended to stop the person passing secrets, but that was not part of his job.

"I don't have access to Ambassadors, Sir Phillip, so I am a bit confused as to how I can help."

"That is where your partner comes in."

Partner?

"I have worked before with an agent who speaks, reads and writes seven languages. Fortunately for us, one of those languages is German."

Seven languages? Bloody hell. The man must be a genius. Dante was lucky he handled English and a bit of French when pressed.

"Have you come up with a way the two of us can work together? If this agent speaks the language, where do I come in?"

Sir Phillip opened his mouth to answer when the door behind Dante opened. "Ah, here she is now."

She? She? She?

Dante almost came up out of his chair. In fact, he did come up out of his chair since a lady had entered the room. This—agent—smiled at him and gracefully took the chair alongside him. She nodded at Sir Phillip and Dante continued to stand like a moron, gaping at her.

The woman was about his age. And beautiful. Shiny, deep brown hair had been fastened in a no-nonsense bun at the back of her neck. Her flower-trimmed straw hat was tied under her lovely chin with a wide net ribbon. Chocolate brown eyes viewed him, taking in his countenance and apparently finding him wanting.

The form-fitting blue and white striped dress went all the way up to her neck, with the sleeves down to her wrists. Unfortunately, she could have been naked for the reaction his body was having.

A slight smile decorated her plush mouth. She offered a delicate cough which startled him enough that he landed in his seat with a thump.

Sir Phillip cleared his throat. "Miss Lydia Sanford, may I make known to you Mr. Dante Rose."

She reached her hand out. He looked at it for a few seconds as if it were a snake ready to strike.

"Good afternoon, Mr. Rose," she said. Her voice was smooth as French brandy and lower than most young ladies' her age.

"Dante?" Sir Phillip said.

He straightened and pulled himself together. He took Miss Sanford's soft warm gloved hand in his and gave it a shake. He looked up into her face and she was still grinning at him.

This would not work. He turned to Sir Phillip. "I don't understand. While I admit I am impressed that Miss Sanford can speak six languages—"

"seven," Miss Sanford added in her melodious voice.

"—I don't see how you intend for us to work together."

Sir Phillip leaned back. "Miss Sanford is active in London's Polite Society. She is invited to the best social events. Our Ambassador attends almost all of them. I firmly believe he is our man and meeting his contacts at those events. With the two of you attending as a courting couple, you will be in a position to do enough—snooping shall we say—to gather the information we need."

Dante sprang from his chair as if shoved from behind. "A courting couple!"

Miss Sanford merely nodded at Sir Phillip as if this were all just fine and dandy with her. He on the other hand had no intention of presenting himself as a suitor to this woman. To any woman.

Sir Phillip looked up at him over the top of his spectacles. "Is there a problem, Mr. Rose?"

Shite. When Sir Phillip called him Mr. Rose, he knew he was in deep. None of the brothers had ever turned down an assignment since their father had also been an undercover agent and instilled in his sons the duty to serve their country in whatever way they could.

Dante ran his finger around the inside of his neckcloth which had grown tighter since this woman had entered the room. Why the devil couldn't his partner be a man, or if it must be a woman, why not someone old enough to be his mother? Or grandmother?

And what the devil was the scent coming from her that smelled like flowers?

He cleared his throat. "It is merely that I have never worked with a woman before. In fact, if you recall, I rarely work with a partner."

Miss Sanford leaned toward him. "I hope you don't have concerns about working together simply because I am a woman?"

Should he be honest or lie? "Not at all, Miss Sanford."

Lying worked because although she smirked, she leaned back in her chair, resting her delicate hand on the knob of the parasol that matched her hat, and didn't respond.

Sir Phillip clapped his hands together. "Excellent. I think this will be a beneficial arrangement."

A rather inconvenient arrangement for me.

If word got out that he was courting a young woman, he would be forced to curtail, *bloody hell*, even stop his thoroughly enjoyable carnal pursuits. He and celibacy were not friends. He cleared his throat. "How long do you foresee this arrangement lasting?"

Sir Phillip grinned. "That depends entirely on you two. Bring me information that I need, and the assignment ends." After studying them both for a few moments, he stood. "I suggest the two of you go for tea somewhere and make your plans. Miss Sanford will have a list of upcoming events that the two of you will attend."

Being summarily dismissed, they both stood and left the room, Dante keeping his distance from the woman. They made their way outside and stood on the pavement and turned to face each other.

"Do you have a carriage, Mr. Rose? If not, I have mine available."

"Yes. I have a carriage, Miss Sanford." When her brows rose, he realized his voice was not at all pleasant. "I apologize. I will be happy to escort you to tea and you may dismiss your driver. I will see that you are delivered home unharmed."

She dipped her head and turned to address the man who hovered near her. After speaking with him, he nodded and climbed onto the top of the carriage. Miss Sanford walked right up to him and placed her arm in his. "I am ready."

Perhaps she was ready, but he wanted to hightail it out of London. Hell, right now the Americas were looking good. She swung her parasol to and fro as they strolled, almost as if they were a courting couple.

Oh, God.

Once they were settled in his carriage, and Dante had given instructions to the driver to take them to a small tea shop where he was unknown, he settled back and studied his *partner* and scowled at her. "Why are you not married?"

"Why are *you* not married?" she snapped.

He huffed. "I'm a man."

"And I am a woman." She stuck her cute little nose in the air. "Now that we have established something that is patently obvious to any observer, why do you care if I am married or not?"

"You are a beautiful woman."

"And you are a handsome man. Alas, I find we are back to my question to you. Why are *you* not married?"

Ignoring the query once again, Dante said, "You should be under the care of a doting husband with several children clinging to your skirts, not working a dangerous assignment for the Home Office."

She waited for several seconds and he could almost see the steam coming from her ears. "I see. Since I am a mere *woman*, all I am good for is producing children and pandering to a husband, despite my talents, intelligence or skills."

Dante waved his hand. "I did not say that."

"Then what, exactly, did you say?"

"I asked why a beautiful woman like you is not married. You must be an age to be considered on the shelf."

Miss Lydia Sanford's face grew red, and she drew in a deep breath. He watched her attempt to control her temper, her eyes flashing and her bosom heaving. He could not take his eyes off her.

She was magnificent.

And major trouble.

Bloody hell. This was going to be the worse assignment he ever worked.

---

2

*L*ydia had to tamp down the strong urge to wallop the arrogant Mr. Rose over his head with her parasol. If she weren't afraid of breaking it—it matched her hat so nicely—she would have done it.

She drew herself up. "Mr. Rose, we need to work together. Unless, of course you wish to disappoint Sir Phillip and back out of the commitment rather than work with a *woman*. I suggest we learn to get along. If we are to fool Society into believing that we are courting, you must refrain from insulting me, since I am afraid the bit of Irish in my blood will draw unnecessary notice to how much I dislike you."

He reared back, appearing genuinely surprised. "Dislike me? All women love me."

"You arrogant nodcock. I am sure the ladies fall all over themselves to garner your attention. However, I am not one of them. You are the owner of a gambling club, a rake, and a supercilious individual."

"Ah, you forgot bastard, as well."

That stopped her cold. She glared at him. "I am assuming you are not adding to my list of insults, but meant your parents were not married. I did not know that, nor do I care. I judge a person on how they behave, not their beginnings. However, based on your behavior, I agree to add bastard to my list of adjectives."

Just then the carriage pulled up to the front of a small tea shop. One that Lydia had visited many times before. As she gathered her things, the driver jumped down from his perch and opened the door. Dante put his hand out to stop her from alighting and left the vehicle first. He turned and held out his hand, his eyebrows raised.

Ah, a dare. Well, she would not give into pettiness. She smiled brightly and reaching out with all the elegance and grace of her station in life, delicately placed her gloved hand in his. Warm and strong. She almost stumbled at the contact, then reminded herself there was nothing in the dastardly man's hand with which she need concern herself.

He glowered at her and she laughed.

"Ah, Miss Sanford, how lovely to see you." The man at the door welcomed them.

"Thank you, Henri, is my favorite table available?"

"Yes." He looked at Dante. "This way, if you please."

They followed the man to a table next to a window over-looking Queen's Square. Once settled, she chatted with Henri in French while Dante gazed out the window, appearing unin-terested.

"Do you mind if I order for both of us?" she asked.

Dante waved his hand. "Please do, Miss Sanford."

She placed an order for her favorite tea blend as well as French pastries. Thank goodness despite her healthy appetite she was able to maintain her figure. Once Henri left, she cleared her throat. Dante drew his focus back to her, although she had the feeling his attention hadn't wandered, he merely wished to appear indifferent.

"I suggest we have our tea before we begin to plan our strategy."

Dante huffed. "Strategy? You mean what balls or other frivolous Society events we shall attend?" He shook his head.

This was not the first time Lydia worked with a man who resented her being a woman. Well, not exactly that, but more having to rely on a woman as part of the investigation. A pleasant, cheerful person by nature, she refused to allow this man's annoyance to dim her excitement at starting a new assignment.

While attempting to plan how she was going to obtain his cooperation without having the urge to throw something at this head, she studied this man she'd been paired with.

He might have been surprised when she showed up, but she'd known before her arrival who her partner was to be, and what the assignment was. Despite his attempt to fluster her, she was well aware that he was the half-brother of the Earl of Huntington and Mr. Driscoll Rose. Although he was his father's illegitimate son, from what she'd learned he'd been raised right along with his two brothers and given every opportunity they'd received.

Dante and his two brothers owned The Rose Room, an exclusive gambling club in London. While she had no repugnance for gambling, she did uncover that the youngest Rose brother was a bit of a rake, rogue, libertine, or whatever one wanted to call it.

His reputation as an excellent lover was known far and wide among the ladies. Even though he shied away from Society events—either through a lack of interest, or concern about his birth—he was still well-known and admired among the Beau Monde.

She had to admit from a very feminine point of view that the man was unusually handsome. Wavy brown hair, longer than current fashion, was tucked behind his ears. He possessed strong aristocratic features, and deep blue eyes that right now were still focused on Queen's Square. His form was perfectly male, something she was sure had the ladies swooning at his feet.

Not that he affected her. Not at all.

"Ah, merci." She leaned back as a waiter placed a teapot, two cups and saucers and a tray of sweets on the table. Once he left, she said, "How do you like your tea?"

"With brandy."

She sighed. He was behaving like a spoiled little boy. She would not allow this.

"Mr. Rose." Something in her voice had him turning toward her with raised brows. She could feel her face beginning to flush. "I do not care if you are annoyed. I do not care if you wish to behave like a spoiled urchin. I am a professional, and I was under the impression after my conference with Sir Phillip that you were one as well. So far you have done nothing to confirm that assurance."

The reprehensible man had the nerve to smile at her. He dipped his head as she picked up the teapot. "You are correct, Miss Sanford. I have been behaving like an ass." He looked up at her with an air of remorse that she didn't believe for one moment. Probably another way to maneuver his way under a lady's skirts.

"I assume since you are a professional that my language doesn't disturb you?" he continued.

Oh, how she wished to hit him over the head with the teapot. She raised her chin. "I prefer good manners, Mr. Rose. To my way of thinking that means polite conversation, which does not include coarse words."

She poured his tea and since he hadn't answered her question, she pushed the cup and saucer in front of him. Let him fix it himself. She offered her own bright smile. "However, I must agree with your assessment. You have been behaving like a bloody ass." She smiled and politely poured her own tea.

Dante threw his head back and laughed so hard he drew attention to them from the other customers. "Miss Sanford, I believe we will get along just fine."

She dipped her head and took a sip of tea.

* * *

DANTE PUT a drop of cream and a teaspoon of sugar into his tea, still smiling at the set-down Miss Sanford had given him. He hated being wrong, but it appeared this woman was not what he'd expected.

When he'd first seen her, he'd been sure her only contribution to the assignment would be her knowledge of languages. Otherwise, he'd expected her to be merely a bit of fluff on his arm to garner invitations to where he would conduct the investigation.

He might hate being wrong, but he was wrong. This woman was not going to allow him to lead her around, merely asking her to translate something. She had fortitude and determination. This assignment might just work.

He watched her delicate hands pour tea, fix her own cup, select two pastries to add to her own plate, all the time ignoring him. It was up to him to smooth things over between them.

"Miss Sanford," he began. "Perhaps we need to start over. I must admit I was stunned by Sir Phillip presenting me with a female partner. 'Twas not something I was expecting."

"Clearly."

"However, I am anxious to proceed with the assignment, as I am sure you are as well. I have a business to run and no doubt you have other interests to take care of as well." There. That should do it to smooth her ruffled feathers. Just to make certain he'd done the right thing, he smiled at her.

Miss Sanford grinned back. "Don't try that on me, Mr.

Rose. That smile all of the ladies in London are familiar with is not going to sway me." She took a sip of tea. "However, I accept your apology—" She stopped. "I assume that was an apology?"

He nodded.

"Excellent. I suggest we finish our tea and then begin our plan."

They were even able to have polite conversation while they enjoyed their tea. The typical subjects of weather and road conditions took up some of the time, as well as observations on those strolling past the window.

Once the waiter had cleared their things away, Miss Sanford whipped out two pieces of paper from her reticule. "I have a list here—actually two lists of the same events—for which I have accepted invitations. In case you are wondering, I have already mentioned when I sent my acceptance that I will be escorted by a friend."

He lowered his eyelids and tilted his lips up in a soft half-smile. "Is that what we are, Miss Sanford. Friends?"

"Stop that!"

He jumped. "What?"

She waved her finger at him and spoke in a heated whisper. "I am not one of your potential conquests, sir. I am here to do a job with you. I want to be treated with respect. If you want our pretend courtship to appear real, then save your heated looks and lazy smiles for when we are at social events."

"Yes, ma'am," he snapped. This was probably not the best time to tell her that when she grew angry like that, with her eyes flashing and her bosoms heaving, everything male in him emerged and all the methods he'd honed over the years to placate a woman and get her into a more amorous mood rose up.

She gave a curt nod. "Just so." She slid one of the pieces of paper across the table. "Here is your list. I have noted the type of event, so you may dress appropriately, the date and time. I will expect you to arrive at my home in your carriage to escort me. If you can arrange to use the Earl's carriage, that would be even better."

"And the Ambassador will be at all these events?"

"As far as I know, yes. He is known to converse in French, German, Spanish and English. Since he spent part of his childhood in Russia, he has been known to slip into that tongue if he feels he's being overheard."

"And those are all languages you are familiar with?" Dante let out a low whistle. "Which is why you were selected for this assignment."

She nodded.

"Sir Phillip mentioned seven languages. What else?"

Without any sort of superciliousness, she rattled off, "Italian and Arabic."

Beautiful, charming, intelligent and gracious—when not goaded. Yet she came out with swear words he would never expect to hear uttered from that sweet, plush mouth. He had to admit she fascinated him.

"Tell me about yourself."

Her head jerked up from where she was studying the list. "What do you mean?"

Dante leaned forward. "I have never met anyone, man or woman, who could speak seven languages. The best educated men I know can't handle more than three."

"Perhaps it is time you moved onto higher circles." She sniffed.

"Touché, Miss Sanford." He gave her a slight salute. "How does a beautiful woman such as yourself end up working for the Home Office on secret assignments, able to speak seven languages?"

Miss Sanford sighed. "Please don't refer to my looks, Mr. Rose." She circled her face with a finger. "What you see here I had nothing to do with. The good Lord provided me with this face and body. I, on the other hand, took the brain he gave me and used it for more than *ton* gossip, and discussions on the latest fashions."

"You must have been a pariah among the other young ladies."

"To some extent. However, much to my disgrace, when I made my debut several years ago, I took on the persona of the typical giggly, blushing, fan-waving young lady."

"And?"

"I hated myself." She looked out the window and he swore there were tears in those beautiful chocolate brown eyes. "One gentleman with the brain of a sheep offered for me. Fortunately, my father was inclined to allow me a say in who I married. I turned him down. As I did more than ten after him."

Another low whistle from Dante.

She took a deep breath and looked back at him. "It was then that I decided marriage and the typical *ton* wife existence was not for me. My father was friends with a man who knew Sir Phillip. Sworn to secrecy, I was permitted a visit with the man."

She shrugged. "The rest is clear to you, I am sure. I now work on secret assignments. Mostly by myself, but on occasion, as now, with a partner."

"Who is your father?"

"The Viscount Sterling. He is a wonderful man. My mother passed away shortly after I refused my tenth offer of marriage. Father ceased at that point to insist that I attend Society events. However, I do keep up with it because I enjoy being there, as long as I am not considered on the Marriage Mart."

"You, Miss Sanford, are an amazing woman."

Much to his surprise and pleasure she blushed. This woman had a spine of steel and for the first time in his life he was interested in a woman for reasons other than her body. Not that he wouldn't thoroughly enjoy taking her to bed, but she was right. There was so much more to her than her face and form.

He looked down at the paper she'd placed in front of him. "I see the first event is a garden party." He looked up and smiled. "I shall try very hard not to groan."

Miss Sanford laughed. "Yes, that is probably not the best event to begin with since I assume you abhor Polite Society, and garden parties are the worst, but the Ambassador and his assistant will both be there, and there is a chance that it is his assistant who is acting as a messenger between the Ambassador and Germany."

"It sounds like you've started this assignment before today." He hoped he didn't come across as petulant.

"Actually, yes. Sir Phillip spoke to me about it last week, and I spent the time from then until now doing some pre-investigation of my own."

"Which you, of course, will share with me." She might be beautiful and intelligent, but he would not be led around by the nose working with her on this assignment.

"Of course."

He tucked the list into his pocket and called for the bill. After making payment, they strolled to his carriage where she gave the driver her home direction.

She told him a bit about the Ambassador that she had learned, and he took notes with the small pad and pencil he always carried with him to meetings with Sir Phillip.

Soon the carriage rolled to a stop in front of a luxurious townhouse in Mayfair. "Your father's home, I assume?"

"Yes. Although he is quite lenient and forward-thinking, he will not permit me my own residence." She smiled and every bit of common sense he ever possessed flew from his head. He reached over to take her hand and when she leaned forward, he pulled her closer and covered her mouth with his.

She was sweet and tender. Warm and moist. Her mouth

tasted like tea and honey. At first, she remained stiff, then she firmly planted her hands on his chest and shoved him back.

The crack from her palm firmly meeting his cheek could no doubt be heard in Grosvenor Square. Without his assistance, she climbed from the carriage and stormed up the steps, her parasol swinging, and her hips swaying.

So. That went well.

3

*D*ante looked up from the newspaper he was reading when Hunt walked into the private dining room on the upper floor of the Rose Room.

"What are you doing here? I thought dragging me away from domestic bliss was necessary because you were on an assignment for Sir Phillip." Hunt headed to the sideboard and poured coffee, then loaded up his plate with breakfast items.

"I am on assignment. This afternoon I am cursed with attending a garden party and since I'm assuming there will be no more than a few dainty edibles available I thought to fill up on real food first."

Hunt sat and shook out his napkin. "A garden party? It appears I was indeed dragged away from home for no reason. What sort of assignment is this?"

Even though they were alone in the dining room, Dante lowered his voice. "Matters that the Crown prefer not to be known have been passed along to Germany. The German Ambassador himself is under suspicion. Since there is reason to speculate that it is at social events where he gathers his information, we are attending as many as we can."

"We?" Hunt's brows rose.

Dante shrugged, attempting to make it appear that he was unconcerned about the assignment and that there was a woman involved. Knowing Hunt, he would not let the matter go until he was fully cognizant of the facts. "I am working with a woman who is well known and received by Polite Society and the recipient of numerous *ton* invitations. She is my entrance to the various events."

"Sir Phillip is using a debutante on such a delicate matter?"

"Not precisely."

Hunt leaned back in his chair, arms crossed, his food forgotten as he examined his youngest brother with something akin to delight and curiosity. Apparently Dante had not done a good enough job of hiding his angst with the situation. "Then tell me, brother. Who is this woman?"

"Miss Lydia Sanford, Viscount Sterling's daughter, apparently does work for Sir Phillip, also. She is beyond the debutante age. I would guess she is close to her mid- twenties."

"Surprising. Both the fact that she is from the Upper Crust, and a female. She must be an unusual woman."

Dante sighed and ran his palm down his face. "She speaks, writes, and reads seven languages. English, Spanish, Italian, German, Russian, French and Arabic."

Hunt studied him with his jaw slack. He shook himself and smiled. "Ugly as sin, I assume. A body not worth looking at?"

"Young, beautiful and possessing a very distractible body."

His brother burst into gales of laughter. "Good luck on this one."

Despite Dante's scowl, his ass of a brother continued to laugh, wiping his eyes with his handkerchief, shaking his head.

"Have I ever told you how happy it makes me to be such a source of amusement for you?"

Driscoll and Amelia entered the room, hands joined as if they were afraid of losing each other on the short walk from their carriage to the dining room. "What's so funny?" Driscoll said.

Dante stood and pushed his chair in. "Hunt, why don't you fill them in, since you find it so entertaining, and I'll go pick up Miss Sanford?"

Amelia looked at Hunt as she sat. "Who is Miss Sanford?"

Indeed, who was Miss Sanford? As Dante made his way downstairs and outside to the carriage—his, not Hunt's—he pondered that question. Aside from exhibiting quite a wallop, she was everything he abhorred in a woman. Arrogant, condescending, confident, and annoying.

If he'd been attributing those faults to a man, it would make sense, and actually make said man appealing to the ladies. However, Miss Sanford was not a man, and those faults did not sit well on a woman. At least not on a woman he'd ever dealt with before. He'd always favored women who were experienced in the bedroom, enjoyed flirting and dalliances, and were aware of how the game was played between a man and a woman who planned for no commitment.

He doubted the haughty Miss Sanford had ever made it anywhere near a bed, except her own. Dressed in a nightgown up to her neck and down to her wrists, with a white ruffled cap on her head. He shuddered at the image.

As the carriage made its way from the club to Miss Sanford's townhouse, Dante had time to go over the situation. The hours he'd spent the night before doing the same thing had not settled him.

He had no idea how to deal with a female partner, how to pretend a courtship with a true lady, and what the devil one did at these *ton* events.

He climbed from the carriage, adjusted his jacket, and took the steps to the front door two at a time. He dropped the knocker, and the door was opened by a man fashionably dressed for the prior century. The butler wore white knickers, buckled shoes, a deep blue jacket and a wig. He bowed. "Good afternoon, Mr. Rose. Miss Sanford awaits you in the drawing room."

The viscount's home was to be admired. Nothing showy or ostentatious. All the wall coverings, floor coverings and furniture were of excellent taste. The surroundings somehow reflected Miss Sanford, who stood in the center of the drawing room as he entered, offering him a bright smile. No sense of irritation from the liberties he'd taken the last time they were together.

Miss Sanford was apparently not of the grudge-holding female class. A rarity to be sure. He'd been subjected to objects hurled at his head, tears, recriminations, threats, and other dramatics which generally ended when he presented the wronged woman with an expensive piece of jewelry.

Perhaps he should have brought Miss Sanford a book on the Chinese languages in the event she needed smoothing over. He bowed. "Miss Sanford. You are looking lovely this afternoon."

Her smile dimmed a bit. "Good afternoon, Mr. Rose. You are looking *lovely* as well." She might not hold grudges, but she wasn't about to allow any sort of the flirtation by which Dante lived his life.

She waved at the sofa next to her. "Will you have a seat? Before we leave, I think we should go over a few things."

He hated more than anything being out of his element. She knew the *ton*. She knew the languages. She knew how to maneuver around in social events. He refused to be the dummy who walked by her side, only to give her protection and the persona of the besotted beau. "Yes. There are a few things I would like to get straight before we start this investigation."

Miss Sanford dipped her head in acknowledgement.

"Sir Phillip saw fit to have two people work on this assignment. Although I bow to your expertise in languages and how to move about in Polite Society, I have no intention of sitting back and watching you work."

When she merely continued to look at him, he continued. "Foremost, my job is to keep you safe—"

She held up her hand. "I don't need—"

He held up *his* hand. "You do. That is one thing I will not compromise on. Despite your feeling of being in control, there are circumstances we might encounter which will require a bit more strength than cursing someone in Arabic."

She actually smiled.

He continued. "If there is to be any snooping or other potentially dangerous activities, I will do those."

"No." She took in a deep breath. "I can do more than translate. I've been on investigations where I've had to snoop. I've even been on an investigation where I had to attempt to seduce a man."

His heart dropped to his stomach. "No. That will not be allowed. Never. Not at all. Did you hear me say no?"

She smiled again. "I did. Aside from my other talents, my hearing is quite strong."

"There will be no seduction. Nor attempts at it. If anyone is to do seducing, it will be me."

"Of the Ambassador? My goodness, based on your reputation, who would have known you had those inclinations?"

He jerked and his lips tightened. "That is not what I meant." He waved his hand around. "Never mind. There are other issues to discuss."

Miss Sanford raised her chin. "Yes. It is now my turn to make demands."

* * *

LYDIA WAS QUITE tired of Mr. Rose laying down rules and ignoring her ability to contribute to the assignment in ways other than translating. However, in her experience, starting off with a friendly, positive manner always worked best. "I understand your concerns, Mr. Rose. I also concede that since I have no intention of following through on an attempted seduction, that might not be the best way to gain answers."

He snorted.

"I will ignore that rude sound you just made and continue. I am able to snoop as well as the next agent of the Home Office, and in the past, I've uncovered vital information that way. However, instead of debating who has the best methods of uncovering information, I suggest I offer you some suggestions about a garden party."

She grinned when he groaned.

"Firstly, if we are to pretend a courtship, it would be wise if you stayed by my side as much as possible. Also, at these sorts of events, there is little formality. We will be free to stroll the grounds, speak with whomever we choose and partake of the refreshments. The most important thing, of course, is to keep our eye on the Ambassador and see who he speaks with."

He nodded and stood. "I suggest we leave."

She stood and shook out her skirts. She'd spent the night before tossing in her bed, thinking about pretending a courtship with Mr. Rose. Ever since the kiss he subjected her to and her automatic response, she'd had to tell herself she had no interest whatsoever in the man in a romantic way.

It hadn't been easy. A renowned flirt and rogue, she would have to protect herself from his attentions. She huffed as they settled in his carriage. He thought to protect her from harm.

Who would protect her from him?

The ride was silent, and for the first time in her social life she felt a bit uneasy arriving at the garden party. It had been years since she had an escort to an event. Since she'd given up pretending to be on the husband hunt, and no longer needed to have a chaperone following her about, she preferred to arrive in her own vehicle, by herself. And leave the same way.

Having her own carriage was best since Mr. Rose was not the first man she'd been forced to slap. Or do other things that prevented further debauchery.

She glanced over at him. There was no way to tell if he felt any apprehension about this, even though he was not a normal guest at *ton* events. He sat relaxed, his foot resting on his other knee, staring out the window. "Do you know what the German Ambassador looks like?" he asked.

"I do. I've met him several times in the past year or so. He is a large man, with a dark mustache that covers his entire upper lip. He appears to be forever dodging his assistant, or secretary, I'm not sure which. A weasel of a little man, with beady eyes, that makes my skin crawl."

"Here we are," Mr. Rose said as the vehicle came to a rolling stop.

Once the door was opened by the driver, Mr. Rose stepped out and turned to assist her. He tucked her arm securely against his side and gave her a wink and his notorious lazy smile. She hated the warm feeling that ran through her at his actions.

"No need to play the part until we have an audience," she said from the side of her mouth.

"Dress rehearsal," he returned.

"Miss Sanford, I am so happy you have decided to join us." Lady Benson, their hostess for the afternoon, walked up to them, her hands extended. They offered each other air-kisses.

Lydia turned to Mr. Rose. Before she could say a word, Lady Benson flushed a light pink and she smiled at him.

"My goodness, Dante. I never expected to see you here. I'd given up on sending you invitations to my little gatherings ages ago." She tapped him on the arm with her fan.

Dante? She knew him by his Christian name?

Mr. Rose bowed over her extended hand. "It is a delight to see you again, Lady Benson."

Her raised brows and slight smirk after glancing at Lydia said a lot about his formality. After a few seconds of silence, their hostess said, "Let me show you where the others have gathered." She took Mr. Rose's other arm and led them along a lovely stone pathway, around the side of the house to a beautiful garden in the rear. She chatted with him the entire time, flirting, casting sultry looks, and generally behaving as though they'd had some sort of secret between them.

Lady Benson had been married for two years.

Things did not improve when they walked up the steps to the patio. Several women moved from various parts of the patio to where she and Mr. Rose stood. Lady Benson continued to hold onto his arm as if she planned to faint and would need his strong arm as support.

It didn't take long for one of the women to edge Lydia aside and grasp his other arm. Exclamations of joy and surprise burst forth from giggling, flirting women, enough to turn Lydia's stomach.

Well, bloody hell.

There would be no conducting an investigation if her *partner* were to be surrounded by adoring females everywhere they went.

The worst part was the man was enjoying himself. He laughed, flirted, and allowed inappropriate suggestions to be tossed in his direction, until she was ready to slam him over the head with something handy and hard. Did he not remember they were supposed to be pretending a courtship?

She moved farther behind him and stabbed him in the back with the point of her parasol.

"Ouch." Mr. Rose jumped as did the two females hanging onto his arms. He turned and took one look at her and immediately released his admirers. He reached his hand out. "Miss Sanford, please join us."

Join them? Join *them?*

She had no idea how severe the look was she tossed him, but he immediately took her arm and the women backed up. Lord, she was coming across as a shrew. Rather than chase the women away, it would be best to join them, as he said, but make certain they knew he'd escorted *her* to the garden party.

'Twould be a very difficult investigation unless she made some things clear from the start. She looked up at Mr. Rose with what she hoped was not the anger she felt, but with affection. "I believe I would like a stroll in the lovely garden, Mr. Rose."

He bowed. "Of course, my dear."

The number of raised brows and gasps at his comment smoothed her feathers. Not that she cared if he flirted with these women. He could do that all day and night if he chose, but they were here to perform a job and spending his time bantering with every female in the place would not get the assignment done.

She was far above flirting. She did not wish to act the simpering, eyelash-batting, arm clinging woman between the schoolroom and the grave.

He took her arm and they moved away from the gathering, with a few of the women suggesting they would like a stroll in the garden, too, when he was finished with her.

They made their way down the steps and onto the continuation of the pathway. Mr. Rose leaned close to her ear. "Jealous, were you?"

She gasped. "Of course not. I don't care how many women throw themselves at you."

Mr. Rose looked forward, patted her hand, and smiled. "I think you *were* jealous."

Oh, the man was insufferable. He was turning this investigation into a—well she had no idea what, but certainly not what they were here for. "Not at all. I assure you."

He smirked.

She stabbed his foot with the point of her parasol.

He grimaced.

They continued their stroll.

4

The garden party unearthed no clues, since the Ambassador did not appear, although Lydia had told him she'd been assured he would attend. After a very stress-filled afternoon, with ladies attempting to shift his attention from Lydia to them, and the steam coming from Lydia's ears, Dante was more than ready to give up this foray into Polite Society and return to the sanity of his club.

Attempting to look disinterested, Lydia kept her eyes on her lap, smoothing her skirts as the carriage rode away from the Benson townhouse. "Do you always get such an overwhelming reception when you attend these affairs?"

Dante laughed. "I do not attend these affairs. I believe I told you before, I avoid them at all costs."

She looked up at him, more with amazement than anger. "You never attend *ton* events?"

"No. I find them a waste of my time."

"Yet, every woman in that garden party knew you." She raised her chin. "And I dare say more than a few knew you in the Biblical sense, as well."

Dante didn't know whether to laugh or blush. Something

he never did. "I don't know what you think of me, but I must tell you my real life doesn't measure up to my reputation. You forget I own and run a business. I don't have as much time for philandering as most people think."

She looked sideways at him and smirked. "Lady Benson is married."

"Yes, that is true. To Lord Benson. For about two years now, I believe."

"Why did she seem so friendly with you?"

Dante leaned back, both amazed and amused at how upset Miss Sanford seemed to be with him. "Yes. She and I enjoyed a short relationship."

Miss Sanford huffed. "And what did her husband think of that?"

He shrugged. "Nothing, since she was not married then. She was a respectable widow at the time and lonely." He leaned forward and looked her in the eye. "I do not dally with married women. Despite what you and most likely everyone else thinks, I think marriage vows are just that—vows. Not to be broken."

She narrowed her eyes, a look of disbelief on her lovely face. "Are you saying if you took a wife, you would be faithful?"

"Of course." He leaned back again, resting his foot on his other knee. "Which situation would never exist since I will never take a wife."

Miss Sanford turned her attention to the busyness on the outside pavement as the carriage moved through traffic. "I understand, since I feel the same way."

"You would not take a wife, either? How interesting."

Her mood switched from somber to laughter. "You know what I mean." She shifted in her seat, getting more comfortable. "As much as you might think marriage is not for you, can you imagine being a woman and knowing that you would be 'owned' by your husband? You cannot sign legal papers, open a bank account, start a business, or even decide where you want to live without your husband's permission."

"I must admit I never thought of that, but you are correct. Which is why if I ever had a sister or daughter in my care, I would make quite sure the man she married was an honorable man who would not treat her like a possession."

Miss Sanford's mouth dropped. "How very forward-thinking of you, Mr.

Rose. I must admit I am impressed with our conversation so far."

"You sound amazed that I am not the monster you thought I was."

She shook her head. "I didn't think you a monster, but based on what I've heard, you are a rogue who broke women's hearts."

"Again, not true. Before I start a relationship with a woman, I make it quite clear that nothing will be permanent. Therefore, no so-called broken hearts."

"Then you never intend to fall in love."

His laughter could probably be heard outside on the pavement. "Love is for young ladies' romance novels. And my two brothers." He mumbled the last part, not even sure why he shared that bit of information.

"What was that you said? I missed it."

Dante cleared his throat. "I said love is for my two brothers."

"Do tell." She offered a bright smile. "I know very little about your brother Driscoll, but I know the Earl of Huntington married a couple of years ago. I must admit it was quite a surprise to most of the ladies who had hopes."

"But not you?" He grabbed the strap hanging next to his head as the carriage jockeyed over bumps in the road.

"No. I happen to like your brother very much, but I had absolutely no *tendre* for him."

It was certainly time to stop this ridiculous conversation. Why were they discussing marriage, love, and other nonsense when they had an investigation to conduct? Another reason why teaming up a man and a woman for an assignment was not a good idea.

Fortunately, they arrived at the Sterling Townhouse before things got more absurd. Dante climbed out first and turned to assist Miss Sanford. As they walked up the steps, he asked, "When is our next event?"

"I gave you a list."

He sighed. "Yes, I know. However, might you allow me this little misstep and tell me?"

She turned toward him as they reached the top step and the front door opened. The same anachronistic butler stood there. "Good afternoon, Miss Sanford."

"Good afternoon, James." She turned back to Dante. "Tomorrow evening there is a ball at Mr. and Mrs. Lenard's home right outside of London. I will check again to make certain the Ambassador is attending before I waste your time." She softened her words with a slight smile. "Good day, Mr. Rose."

He was beginning to believe this entire assignment was a waste of his time.

* * *

THE FOLLOWING EVENING, Lydia studied herself in the looking glass on her dressing table. She backed up until she could see her entire body. The deep blue satin gown fit her perfectly. The neckline was sufficiently low enough to cause interest, without being immodest. Of course, as an older single woman, most likely considered on the shelf, she had some freedom in what she could wear.

Her maid, Alice had arranged her hair into an intricate style with pearls woven throughout. She turned one way, then the other, assessing herself and when she realized what she was doing, she groaned and stepped away from the mirror.

She had never spent so much time on her attire when she'd attended these events. Not that she didn't care about how she looked, but never before was she so particular.

A knock on her bedchamber door made her start with surprise. Why were her nerves so frazzled tonight? This was just another assignment out of the dozen or so she'd done before.

"Yes."

Alice opened the door and stuck her head in. "Mr. Rose has arrived. I put him in the drawing room."

"Thank you, Alice. I will be right down. Please offer Mr. Rose a drink."

"Yes, Miss Sanford."

She slid her gloves on, picked up her reticule and shawl and left the room. She took a deep breath outside the drawing room and nodded for James to open the door.

Mr. Rose stood in the center of the room, sipping on a brandy. She offered a bright smile and demanded her heart to slow down. It did not listen.

He was dressed in formal black except for his silver waistcoat and silver and black striped necktie. As usual, part of his hair fell forward, and he pushed it behind his ear. He studied her over the top of his brandy snifter, those blue piercing eyes going from her feet to her head, leaving a wake of heat in its path.

"I will not comment on your looks, Miss Sanford lest you chastise me again. However, is it acceptable if I mention how lovely your brain looks?"

The laugh burst forth from her mouth before she even gave it a thought. The man was a scoundrel. "Thank you, I think."

He sauntered across the room, like a predator toward its

victim and took her hand in his, turned it over and placed a soft kiss there. She felt the heat through her glove.

Oh, he was good.

"May I pour you a drink before we leave?" he said, his eyes still boring into hers.

"Yes." The word came out like a frog had taken up residence in her throat.

This nonsense had to stop. The man was a known flirt and philanderer. She would not permit him to use his wiles on her when there was an assignment to conduct. She said, "Actually, no thank you." She swung her matching blue satin shawl around her shoulders and raised her chin. "I believe it is time we left."

The look on his face told her he knew exactly what she was about. "Of course." He downed the brandy, and before he could move to her side, she hurried from the room.

She gritted her teeth at the sound of his chuckle.

She'd managed to pull her libido under control by the time the carriage came to a rolling stop in front of the Lenards' home. Since it was a longer ride with the residence located outside London proper, they'd spent part of the time with her describing the Ambassador and his assistant.

With this being a larger gathering than the garden party, it was important for them both to know for whom they were searching.

They followed the crowd in a queue as they made their way from their carriages to the house. Lydia had just turned to ask Mr. Rose a question when a woman walked up to them. "Dante, darling. I heard you attended Lady Benson's garden party, but I told Miss Howard I would not believe Mr. Dante Rose would attend a *ton* event unless I see him with my own eyes."

"Well, here he is, Lady Rockford," Lydia said, her eyes narrowed, trying very hard not to sound as annoyed as she felt.

"Oh, hello Miss Sanford. I didn't see you there."

Clearly.

To Mr. Rose's credit, he placed his hand over hers where it rested on his arm. Lady Rockford took notice, her brows raised. "Is there a particular reason why you have deigned to join our gatherings?"

"I find with Miss Sanford by my side they are not quite so trying."

Lydia almost swallowed her teeth. He was playing his part so successfully that Lady Rockford actually reared back. "Do tell." She lowered her eyelids.

Just then the queue began to move again, and she tapped him on his arm with her fan. "Just be sure to see me inside so you can add your name to my dance card, darling." With a cold look at Lydia, she swept her skirts away and walked up to another woman in the line. They soon had their heads together.

"Well done, Mr. Rose."

He looked down at her. "I hope you know how much that cost me."

"Oh, goodness. Whatever will the ladies of the *ton* do? They will probably cry themselves to sleep tonight."

"Only tonight, Miss Sanford?" His grin was infectious.

She shook her head at his audaciousness. "If we are to be believed, I think it is time to drop the *Mr. Rose* and *Miss Sanford.* It is time we used Lydia and Dante."

He ran his finger around the inside of his neckcloth. "You are really going to put a dent in my amorous attempts once this assignment is over, Miss Sanford. Rather, Lydia."

She laughed. "I have every confidence that you will have no problems when released from this. You will return to your rogue ways, and the ladies will be more than happy to accept you back into their fold. Or bed."

* * *

DAMN, but he enjoyed bantering with her. *Lydia.*

Most of his past repartee with other women had been sexual in nature, a prelude to bedsport. In some ways it was refreshing to have someone poke a hole in his self-confidence. However, his highly honed bedroom skills told him despite what she professed Miss Lydia Sanford was attracted to him.

There was no doubt in his mind that he was attracted to her. But she being unmarried and most likely innocent, he would not pursue that attraction. Her doting father would come down on him like a ton of bricks if she were compromised in any way.

She seemed to think her father was worldly and forward-thinking, but he'd met enough men with marriage-age offspring to know before they passed from this earth, they all wanted their daughters to remain pure until settled and secure with a husband and home.

With a daughter of Lydia's age, the man most likely kept marriage settlements in the top drawer of his desk, ready to whip out and fill in the blank spaces at a moment's notice. Hell, he wouldn't be surprised if Viscount Sterling had an undated Special License tucked in along with marriage settlements and the local vicar on call.

Dante helped Lydia remove her shawl and handed it to the footman taking outer garments from the guests. Dante did an excellent job of stopping himself from kissing the back of her sleek neck where a few strands of hair rested.

They made their way to the top of the stairs leading to the ballroom below. After the few other guests in front of them had been announced, Lydia handed her invitation to the footman.

"Mr. Dante Rose and Miss Lydia Sanford." The man's voice rang out over the rumble of conversation.

They made their way down the stairs. Dante picked out quite a few of the gentlemen he knew as patrons of the Rose Room. He honestly did not pay attention to the women since he was now in investigation mode. But alas, once they reached the ballroom floor two women approached him.

He never thought he would reach a point in his life when women approaching him became a nuisance. That, however, was precisely how he felt. He grabbed Lydia's wrist. "Let me see your dance card."

He quickly filled in three spaces. Two waltzes and one quadrille. She took the card from his hand and gasped. "You cannot have three dances. That would be scandalous."

"Then we shall walk the perimeter of the room during one of them. I just don't want to spend all night dancing. We have a job to do."

"Dante, dear. Please say you've saved a waltz for me." Miss Adelina Grayson held her card out as did her sister, Miss Grayson."

He bowed and took the cards, filled them in—no waltzes since his were already taken—and before they could start their eyelid flapping and giggling, he grasped Lydia's arm. "I think I could use some champagne." He left the two women and four others gaping as he walked away with Lydia on his arm.

"I'm beginning to think having you escort me to these events so we can conduct an investigation is not going to work," Lydia said.

"It will work, my sweet. We just need to keep ourselves busy, walking, dancing, and visiting the refreshment table." He steered Lydia toward the table against the wall filled with the warm ratafia and lemonade.

Luckily, on their way, he was able to grab two glasses of champagne from a footman's tray and passed one to Lydia. She took one sip and looking over his shoulder, her eyes grew wide. "Ambassador. What a pleasure to see you tonight."

Dante turned and looked into the eyes of the man they'd been searching for. A man who was stealing secrets from England and passing them along to Germany. Tall and robust to the point of straining his jacket buttons, the man irritated him with how his dark dangerous eyes looked Lydia up and down, the lust on his face unmistakable.

"Good evening, Miss Sanford. You look lovely, as always."

Lydia gestured to the man. "Ambassador Schulze, may I present to you Mr. Dante Rose." Dante extended his hand, which the ambassador accepted. "Ambassador. It is a pleasure to meet you outside of the club."

And keep your lustful eyes off Lydia.

---

5

*L*ydia cringed as the Ambassador took her hand in his and kissed the back. She quelled the desire to wipe it off and was grateful she wore gloves. She'd never spent much time in the man's company and decided the worst part of this assignment was not dealing with Dante, but with having to insert herself into the Ambassador's presence until they could discover the traitor passing information to him.

"My dear, you must honor me with a dance." The Ambassador reached for her dance card. Studying it for a minute, he said, "Oh, my good man," he glanced at Dante, "you cannot deprive the rest of us from waltzing with this fascinating young lady by taking up both waltzes."

Lydia had not looked closely at her dance card but was happy to note that of the three dances Dante had filled in, he'd claimed the two waltzes. She answered in relief, "I am so sorry, Ambassador, perhaps one of the quadrilles?"

He shrugged. "If I must." He sounded generally annoyed as he took the small pencil dangling from the dance card and filled in his name. This was obviously a man who controlled his world quite well and was not happy when things did not go his way.

She was torn between asking Dante to give up one of his waltzes in the name of the Home Office, or not, since she didn't particularly want to spend twenty minutes that close to the Ambassador.

Before she could decide, he offered a slight bow. "I must take your leave now, as there are people I must speak with. I will return for our dance." He had the nerve to once again stare at her in such a way that made her skin break into gooseflesh.

Lydia ran her palms up and down her arms. "I don't like that man."

Dante took her arm. "That makes two of us. We must keep our eyes on him without seeming to. I suggest a stroll around the room in the direction he is headed."

They were stopped several times by women wanting Dante to put his name on their dance cards. It seemed every woman who approached them was looking for a waltz. Lydia had reached the point where she found their forwardness amusing. These women seemed almost desperate when Dante did not encourage them. And for that she was grateful.

Another amusing note were the number of gentlemen who requested dances from her. Not that she'd ever been a wallflower, but rarely was her dance card filled for the night as the years passed, and she remained single. Tonight, every dance was spoken for.

Perhaps her escort had something to do with it. Men's need to compete.

"It appears you are popular with the gentlemen, Lydia." Dante placed his hand on her lower back and steered her toward the wall where bottles of champagne were being poured into slim crystal glasses.

She grinned as they wove their way through the crowded

room. "I have never been a wallflower, but over the years the requests for a dance did dwindle."

"Ah, the gentlemen learned you had no interest in pursuing a husband?"

Lydia shrugged as she took the glass of champagne from his hand. "Perhaps. Not all gentlemen are interested in marriage." She waved her glass in his direction. "However, as I grew beyond the blushing debutante age, the gentlemen were more interested in a dalliance."

"Assumptions were made?"

"I believe so. Word had spread that I was an independent, forward-thinking, intelligent woman, not interested in marriage." She glanced up at him over the rim of her glass. "What would your assumption be?"

"I see your point."

Just then the orchestra started up, a lively country dance. Mr. Berger, the man who requested the dance strolled up to her. He put his hand out. "My dance, I believe, Miss Sanford?"

As she strolled away, she saw Dante moving through the crowd. She didn't know if he was headed to a partner for a promised dance, or still keeping his eyes on the Ambassador. It didn't matter since once the dance began, she was taken up with Mr. Berger attempting to converse while switching partners.

Her partner's face grew flushed with the effort of the lively dance and trying to ask her questions about her upcoming week. She dodged as many as she could since she did not wish to spend time riding through the park or strolling on his arm. She smiled a great deal and made motions of not being able to understand him.

Hopefully, once the dance had ended he would be much too out of breath to continue to ask.

Lydia, on the other hand was having a grand time. She'd always enjoyed dancing and her feet moving in time to the music always brought her joy. Dante apparently did have a dance partner since he was only four couples down from her and Mr. Berger.

Dante looked at her. Their eyes met and she stumbled. Mr. Berger reached out and took her arm to steady her. She felt like a fool. She would never fall under that devil's spell. She would never become one of the ladies who practically swooned when he spoke to them.

She would not.

She glanced back again, and he was staring at her, his lips in a slight smile. Stumbling wasn't bad enough, now she felt a blush rise to her face. If she had to follow the Ambassador around twenty-four hours a day, she would do it to end this assignment.

She sniffed. Miss Lydia Sanford did not make a fool of herself over a libertine.

* * *

DANTE TRIED his best to ignore Lydia and keep his eyes on his partner. Earlier, he'd followed the Ambassador around the room until the man claimed his own partner for the dance. Expecting to lounge against the wall until Lydia returned, he was nevertheless coerced into dancing with Lady Wilson's youngest daughter, Miss Kathleen.

The chit was barely out of the schoolroom, and he was amazed that the woman had pushed them together. He would never let a daughter of his anywhere near a man with his reputation.

His current problem was keeping his eyes off Lydia. He'd lost his breath when she'd entered the drawing room when he'd arrived to escort her to the ball. Luckily he was not in the middle of taking a sip of his brandy, or it would have spewed all over him.

If he had to work with a woman, why did she have to look like Lydia? In fact, no woman who could read, write, and speak seven languages should look like Lydia. She should be pale and scrawny from spending all her time indoors translating documents. She should have thick spectacles perched on her nose and look old and wrinkled from bending over books, memorizing sentence structures, conjugating verbs.

The dress his Home Office partner had worn to the garden party had been perfect for the setting and she'd looked wonderful. But this gown, this evening gown, had him ready to drag her back up to her bedchamber and spend the rest of the night in much more pleasurable pursuits.

His mind wandered back to their conversation about the requests she'd received for a dalliance once it had become known she was not interested in marriage. Had she accepted any of the offers? Did he care?

Yes, he cared. If she were open to a liaison, he would be more than happy to accommodate her.

"Don't you agree, Mr. Rose?" Miss Kathleen looked at him with worshipful eyes. Damn. Just what he needed, a girl barely out of nappies developing a *tendre* for him. Another reason he avoided these events.

Too many times in his life he'd agreed to something, not really sure what it was since his mind had been wandering when the question arose. He would not fall into that trap again. "I apologize, Miss Kathleen, but with the music I don't believe I heard you."

"I said riding in Hyde Park in the afternoon is such a lovely way to enjoy the newly arrived summer, is it not?"

Thank the heavens he asked her to repeat her question. Images of him driving the young girl in the park while the entire *ton* looked on was enough to cause him to break out into hives.

"I'm afraid with my commitments, I never have time for

rides in the park." He tried to look sorry, but all he felt was relief. The look of annoyance on her face doubled his relief. When the bloody hell would this dance be over?

He glanced down the line again where Lydia danced with Mr. Berger. She looked over at him and when their eyes met he nearly lost his footing. He frowned, causing her to raise her eyebrows. The neckline on that gown was entirely too low, and he might have to remind Mr. Berger where Lydia's face was because his eyes kept wandering below her chin.

Miss Kathleen was asking him another question and he was ready to walk off the floor. He shrugged and smiled, tapping his ear, hoping that would dissuade her from asking anything else. Mercifully, within minutes the musical piece ended, and he escorted the young girl back to her mother. Mumbling something about needing to see a friend across the room, he bowed and took his leave.

He approached Lydia who stood with two other women, fanning herself. After being introduced to Lady Marion and Miss Parker, he said, "I am up for a drink, what say you?"

"Yes, that would be wonderful." Lydia turned to her two companions. "Would you care to walk with us to the refreshment table?"

They both declined, and he took Lydia's arm. "I think we should have a discussion about your evening gown."

Lydia drew back and turned toward him. "Pardon me? I'm not quite sure what you mean. Or, actually I think I do know what you mean and I want to know why you think you have the right to suggest anything about my apparel?"

Dante ran his finger along the inside of his neckcloth. "I just think if we are to work on an assignment, it might go better if your mode of dress was a little bit more. . ."

She narrowed her eyes. "More what?"

"Subdued." He took her arm again and they continued. "We need to be inconspicuous so we can listen to the Ambassador's conversations. With the attention you are getting, we won't be able to get near him."

"And I suppose all the ladies dropping everything, including themselves at your feet does not garner attention?"

Dante picked up two glasses of warm lemonade and handed one to Lydia, who studied it so long before taking it that he was sure she was about to dump it on his head.

"The Ambassador is interested in you."

"I know."

"I'm not sure if you understand what I mean. He is interested in a certain way."

"Oh for heaven's sake, Dante. Out with it. He wants to bed me."

He should have known better than to attempt to speak with Lydia in anything but explicit terms. "Yes. That is precisely what I meant. The entire time we were in his company his eyes never rose above your neckline."

"Neither did Mr. Berger's." Lydia tossed her head. "I refuse to worry about men who cannot keep their eyes where they belong. And furthermore, there is nothing at all immodest about this gown. In fact, I think it looks quite nice."

Dante downed the rest of his lemonade. "It looks much more than nice," he growled. With a smirk, he added, "Um, your brain that is."

Just then the orchestra started up the first waltz of the evening. Dante took the glass from Lydia's hand and placed it on the table. "My dance, I believe, Miss Sanford?"

Damn, he hated how good she felt in his arms. Warm, soft, with an intriguing scent wafting from her hair. He wanted to glance down to admire what all the rest of the men had been gaping at, but he was quite certain he would get a dressing down after the comments about the Ambassador and Mr. Berger.

No surprise to him, she was light on her feet, followed him flawlessly, and it felt as though they'd danced together for years. He attempted a few twists and turns and she followed perfectly. Even though he hadn't spent time at *ton* events, there was nothing wrong with his dancing skills.

He pulled her in close for a turn and felt her intake of breath. He studied her face and realized she was having thoughts similar to his. Dangerous territory here for him.

"You're holding me too tight." Lydia attempted to push back, but he didn't allow it.

"Crowded dancefloor," he mumbled.

He looked over her head and saw the Ambassador and another man leave the ballroom through the French doors. He maneuvered them past three other couples, swung her around and opened the French doors at the same time.

"What? What are you doing?"

He took her arm in his and leaned close to her ear. "The Ambassador just left through this door with another man."

Dante looked over the balustrade. The two men were strolling the pathway but did not seem to be talking. He moved Lydia in the same direction. "Come."

They walked quickly and quietly. The two men stopped and sat on a stone bench. Dante pulled Lydia along another pathway that seemed to wind directly behind where they sat.

They ended up close enough to hear their exchange. They were speaking, but in a foreign language. Lydia held her finger up to her lips and moved closer. She leaned in and listened, her brows furrowed in concentration. After a few minutes, she backed, up shook her head and moved to return the way they came.

Once they had returned to the main path, she said, "They were speaking German. But it was nothing of importance. All they seemed to be discussing were food and parties. The

Ambassador was comparing events he'd attended in Germany to those here in England."

"That seems to be an odd subject for two men to be talking about, alone, outside a ballroom."

Lydia shrugged. "Perhaps the Ambassador is lonely. It appeared the man with him had just arrived from Germany and was recently assigned to the Embassy here in London. You know how difficult it can be to have any sort of a conversation in a crowded ballroom."

They walked a bit farther until they arrived at a small pergola. They climbed the two steps and settled on a wooden bench. Lydia took in a deep breath, drawing his attention once more to her breasts. "It's so peaceful out here. As much as I enjoy balls and other events, I do try to take a break from the festivities and stroll in the gardens when I can."

The scant moonlight cast a shadow on her face, giving her skin a silver glow. She turned to him, her mouth opened as if to say something. Then she stopped and tilted her head. "What?"

"Nothing." He smiled. "Just this." He pulled her closer and covered her mouth with his. Yes. Just as wonderful as he'd remembered. Her mouth was soft, sweet, warm and moist. When she didn't pull back and smack him in the face again, he took the kiss deeper, nudging her lips to open and accept him fully.

He groaned and pulled her flush against him, feeling her lush breasts pressed up against his chest. Just as things became interesting, a woman's cry rent the air.

*L*ydia followed Dante as he rushed down the two steps from the pergola and headed down the path to where Miss Kathleen sat on the ground, holding her foot and moaning. Young Lord Belford, a lad new to his title, hovered over her.

"What happened?" Dante said looking back and forth between them.

They had begun to gather a crowd when Lydia reached them. She bent over Miss Kathleen, careful to keep the bottom of her gown off the damp grass. "Are you hurt?"

"Yes, I think I twisted my ankle."

Glancing around at a nervous looking Lord Belford, then back to Miss Kathleen, she said, "Where is your mother? You should not be out here alone."

"I wasn't alone," the girl moaned. "I was with Lord Belford."

"That's even worse," Lydia mumbled. She put her hands under the girl's arms and lifted her. She cried as her foot hit the ground. She had obviously damaged her ankle.

"What happened?"

Miss Kathleen wiped a tear from the corner of her eye. "We

were merely strolling and my foot hit a rock and I stumbled and fell.

Apparently Lord Belford hadn't taken very good care of the girl if she went down after a slight stumble. Dante was busy talking to Lord Belford, and from the look on Dante's face, he was offering some sage advice to the young lord about taking innocent young ladies for a stroll in the garden with the entire *ton* a few steps away. More than one hurried wedding had taken place with those conditions. With a pat on Belford's back from Dante, the man turned and made a quick exit from the garden.

"I will fetch her mother," Dante said, also making a fast escape.

Lydia wrapped her arm around Miss Kathleen's back and moved her to a stone bench a few steps from where they stood. She settled next to the girl awaiting Miss Kathleen's mother.

"I must offer advice to you that I'm sure your mother has told you, but maybe coming from me, you might actually listen." She pushed wayward curls back from the girl's forehead that had fallen during her mishap.

"Do not go into gardens with a young man. A stroll on the patio in full sight of the rest of the ballroom is fine. But you are looking for trouble if you wander farther away."

"Lord Belford did nothing wrong," the girl said.

"Perhaps because you weren't here long enough. As I said, you may or may not take heed to my words, but foolish actions can have life-long consequences."

Just then Lady Wilson came flying down the steps to where her daughter sat. "Oh, my dear. Whatever were you doing out here?"

"Just taking some fresh air mother." The girl was smart enough not to mention she was escorted by a gentleman.

Her mother tsked. "Your father has sent for the carriage. He will be here in a thrice to help you."

Dante moved toward Lydia. "I believe this is a good time for us to depart."

"Yes." She took his arm, and they made their way up the steps and through the French doors. Once they located their hostess for the evening, and bid her goodnight, they left and settled into Dante's carriage.

"Not much gained tonight," Dante said as he stared out the window at the darkness. Being outside the City there were few lights, with only the pale moonlight to guide the driver.

"No, that's true. However, I really thought the man who walked out to the garden with the Ambassador might be the one."

Dante shrugged. "Just because they didn't discuss anything of interest to us, there is still the possibility he is our man. If they are both missing Germany, a conversation on the differences between the two countries would seem normal."

"I agree."

Once they grew silent, Lydia's mind wandered back to the kiss they'd shared in the pergola before Miss Kathleen interrupted them. She really should not have allowed that. They were partners in a Home Office assignment. They had a job to do.

She had no interest in any sort of a permanent arrangement with a man. Although she had to admit that as the years continued to pass, the idea of a dalliance did hold appeal. Truthfully, Dante was the first man with whom she'd ever considered such a thing. Could it be because she was older, or because the attraction she felt toward him and he toward her was putting those ideas into her head? But she certainly did not want a husband. Nor did Dante want a wife.

Bringing her mind back to why they were together to begin with, she said, "Our next event is two days from now. It is the musicale at the Price home. I believe their two daughters, Miss Amy and Miss Margaret are performing."

Dante dropped his head in his hand and groaned. He looked sideways at her. "A musicale? How will we eavesdrop there?"

"We can see who approaches the Ambassador, and who he seeks out before and after the event."

"This is by far the hardest assignment I've ever had." He rested his head against the squab and stared at the ceiling.

Lydia drew herself up. "Because I am your partner?"

He rolled his head toward her and offered that irresistible-to-most-women smile. "Not at all, Miss Sanford. I must admit you are better looking—and possess a far better brain, I find I need to add—than any of the other partners I've worked with."

She glowed with his compliment and then scowled. Why did his approval mean so much to her? He was a scoundrel, the possessor of a bad reputation. He owned and operated a gaming club. He was arrogant, supercilious, and dangerous to her.

"I do appreciate the night off, however. My brother will be glad, I am sure, to have my assistance tomorrow night."

Just as the carriage came to a stop in front of her home, she had a wonderful idea. "I have a favor to ask."

Dante stopped as he was reaching for the door. "What is that?"

Lydia cleared her throat. "I would love to see the Rose Room."

"No." He opened the door and stepped out.

She sat stubbornly in her seat while he remained outside. "Why not?"

He reached for her hand and rather than be tugged from the vehicle like a recalcitrant child, she stepped out and took his arm.

"Ladies are not allowed in the club." They started up the steps.

"Why not?"

They reached the top step and the front door opened. "Just

give me a minute, please, James."

The butler nodded and stepped away from the door, leaving it unlatched, but closed.

Dante crossed his arms over his chest. "My brothers and I don't feel it's a proper place for ladies. The only women allowed are those who don't fit that appellation."

"Well. That is certainly unfair."

"Why would you want to see the club?"

Lydia shrugged. "Curiosity. Now that I am older, I find a lot of restrictions placed upon ladies are antiquated."

Dante stood with his hands on his hips. "I can offer a compromise."

"Yes?"

"I will bring you to my club before it opens. You can have a look around.

"No."

His brows rose. "No?"

"No. I want to see it when there are people there. Playing."

The more she thought about it, the more anxious she was to see the place. The Rose Room had a reputation among the *ton* as one of the best clubs in London. Although not a known fact when it first opened, now most everyone was aware that the Earl of Huntington was one of the owners. That had attached quite a bit of notoriety and curiosity to the place.

"Driscoll's wife worked there. As a dealer."

"How did you know that?"

She grinned at his scowl. "I work as a spy, remember?"

Dante offered a very deep and exaggerated sigh. "Very well. Be ready at eight o'clock tomorrow night. I will escort you through the back door and up to the second floor where the offices are. There is an area where you can stand and observe the floor without being seen."

Lydia grinned. "See. There is always a solution to any problem."

Dante rested his hands on her shoulders. "Yes. But the solution to some problems tend to be worse than the problem itself." With those cryptic words he touched his lips briefly to her forehead and hurried down the steps.

* * *

THERE WAS no doubt in Dante's mind that he'd taken leave of his senses almost from the minute he'd first laid eyes upon Miss Lydia Sanford.

Yes, she was beautiful. No, she was not a giggling debutante. Yes, she was smart, bold, witty, and gracious. Had he been in the market for a wife, and she for a husband, they would make an excellent match. But he wasn't, and she wasn't. However, she was certainly worldly enough and old enough to indulge in a brief affair.

He pushed to the back of his mind the thought that an affair with Lydia would not be brief. The fire and passion he felt in her body each time he'd kissed her told him it would take quite a long time to have his fill of her.

If ever.

These thoughts ruminated through his mind the next evening as he made his way up the steps to her townhouse to escort her to the club.

He wondered if he hadn't made a mistake by taking her to his place of business. They should really keep their contact strictly professional and not become involved in any other way. With those mixed feelings, he dropped the knocker on the door and it swiftly opened.

"Mr. Rose, Miss Sanford awaits you in the drawing room. If you would follow me." The strange little butler led him up the stairs to the first floor, then down the corridor to the drawing room.

Lydia sat on a settee sipping a glass of sherry. She stood as he entered. "Good evening. I thought you might want a drink before we left."

Dante nodded and walked to the sideboard where an array of liquor bottles sat. "Ordinarily I do not drink before I work, but since I will not allow a lady to drink by herself. . ."

Once he poured two fingers of brandy into a snifter, he joined her on the settee. Swirling the brown liquid around, he said, "I suggest we travel in your carriage so you can return when you wish. I stay until after the club closes."

Lydia shook her head. "No. If this is to be my only visit to the famous Rose Room, I want to stay all night."

His brows rose.

She blushed. "I mean until the club closes."

Dante took a sip of his drink. "I thought for a minute you knew we had a bedroom there and wished to make use of it." He grinned. "I would be more than happy to join you, of course. Good manners and all that."

Dante wished the words back immediately. He'd just gone through a self-lecture on keeping their relationship on a professional basis. Truth be known, never having a relationship with a woman that did not involve carnal pursuits he was out of his territory, so he was bound to make mistakes.

Lydia finished her sherry and placed the glass on the table in front of her. "I appreciate the offer, Mr. Rose, but I'm afraid I must decline."

"Ah. I am not surprised." He downed his brandy and stood. She turned and headed to the door and he followed her downstairs to the entrance hall, all the time admiring the sway of her lovely backside.

The black satin dress she wore, fitted to her curvaceous body, with small cap sleeves had his mouth watering. Some sort of sparkles had been sewn to the bodice and where the gown wrapped tightly against her stomach to gather in the back into a slight bustle.

Smooth white skin rose above the neckline, calling attention to the beautiful globes and the slim column of her neck. A diamond and onyx necklace rested against her alabaster skin, teasing the tops of her breasts, as well as him. Black feathers decorated her hair, swooping down to barely touch her left ear.

He had the urge to throw one of the rugs under the seat of his carriage over her and carry her into the club, then lock her into the bedroom so no one else would see her. "I will not comment on your gown, which is lovely, but your brain is a bit scant tonight."

She pulled the shawl tighter against her body. "This is a perfectly respectable gown."

"I certainly appreciate it." As did his body which was doing odd things to him. Aside from the instant erection when he walked into the drawing room, his hands itched to caress her soft skin and his mouth craved to plunge his tongue into her sweet mouth and possess her. Completely.

He was certainly grateful she had agreed to remain upstairs in the club, out of sight so she could watch the players. Truth be known, he had a bit of a problem believing this woman would remain unnoticed no matter where she stood.

He'd told the driver to go around to the back of the club when they arrived, even though it was still more than an hour before it opened. Instead of taking her hand in his after he exited the carriage, he reached in, placing both his hands on her waist, and lifted her.

Warmth, softness, and the scent of something exotic had his body once again sitting up and taking notice. He stared into her eyes as he placed her on the ground but didn't release her.

All was lost when she looked up at him under those thick dark eyelashes and licked her lips. With a slight moan, he drew her to him and crushed her against his body.

Lydia raised her hands and cupped his cheeks, urging him to pull her even closer until they were pressed up against each other like canned sardines. Except Miss Lydia Sanford smelled and felt a great deal better.

He pulled away and scattered kisses along her jawline, the enticing column of her neck and the soft sensitive skin under her ear. "You are so beautiful." He leaned back and placed his finger under her chin. "I'll have you know I've never had the desire to bed one of my partners. Until now."

A soft moan escaped her, and she ran her palms up and down his back. He pushed his hips into hers and moved back and forth. A torture to be sure, but he was unable to stop himself.

Lydia's knees seemed to melt, and he had to hold her tighter to keep her from collapsing. After a minute, he drew away. Even though they were behind the building, they did stand outside. The last thing he wanted to do was destroy her reputation. Shortly streams of men would arrive and he needed to get her upstairs and himself under control and in a frame of mind to work.

He pulled away and smiled down at her. The scant moonlight highlighted her moist, plump lips, now swollen from his kisses. "We need to go upstairs, love."

She gazed at him with unfocused eyes.

"Lydia." He took her hand and led her to the back door. "Come."

They made it to the top of the stairs where they encountered Keniel, the club manager. He looked appreciatively at Lydia. "Who have we here?"

Dante's muscles immediately tightened, and his jaw clenched. Keniel was too good looking, and a bit of a rake himself. "Someone you need not concern yourself with," Dante said as he took Lydia's hand and walked her toward the dining room.

Keniel's deep, soft chuckle floated in the air as they moved away.

hey entered a dining room with a sideboard that held an array of food, a pot of tea and one of coffee. Dante waved in that direction. "Several of us eat here before the club opens." He looked down at her. "Are you hungry?"

She shook her head. "No. I've had dinner, but I would like a cup of tea."

"Help yourself."

Once she fixed her tea, she wandered to the dining table with six comfortable looking chairs surrounding it. It was a pleasant room, and even though she wasn't hungry, the aroma from the food on the sideboard was tempting. Dante pulled out a chair for her and took the one across.

Driscoll Rose entered the room and came to an abrupt stop, looking in Lydia's direction. "Good evening, brother. I thought we would not see you for a while."

"We have an evening off, so I thought to come by and help out." Dante gestured to Lydia. "Driscoll, this is Miss Lydia Sanford. My partner. Lydia, my brother and also my partner, Mr. Driscoll Rose."

Lydia smiled. "It is a pleasure to see you again, Mr. Rose. I believe we were introduced at a ball a few years ago. It was the coming out ball for Miss Penelope White."

Driscoll's jaw dropped. "You have an excellent memory, Miss Sanford."

Dante laughed. "One needs an excellent memory to keep seven languages straight."

Driscoll poured a cup of coffee and settled next to Dante. "Something tells me there is a story here."

"Miss Sanford speaks, reads and writes English, French, Spanish, German, Italian, Russian and Arabic." He turned to her. "Did I get that right?

To Lydia's ears Dante almost sounded proud. "Yes. You did."

Driscoll stared at her for a moment, then said, "No Greek?"

The three burst out laughing and Lydia decided this Mr. Rose had a great sense of humor. "No. I'm afraid I need to work on that one."

"Where is your wife?" Dante asked. "I thought Amelia is working on the books while you take on the extra duties."

Lydia placed her teacup in the saucer. "Your wife is the woman who dealt cards for a while here, isn't that correct?"

"Yes." Driscoll scowled.

Lydia tilted her head to the side and regarded him. "Oh, you sound cross."

"I didn't like her working on the game room floor when we were not married, and I forbade it after we married."

Dante glanced at Lydia. "Except Amelia Rose is not someone to be told what to do. She continued to deal at the *vingt-et-un* table until she became with child."

"Ah. When is the babe due to arrive?"

Driscoll's face glowed in such a way Lydia wondered if anyone would ever look like that when speaking of her. It had warmed her to hear the pride in Dante's voice as he recited her accomplishments, but this was different. A babe was something he and his wife had created together.

Then she brought herself up short. She'd made the decision a few years ago to bypass all of that. Marriage, husband and children were not to be her life. She was quite pleased with her life just the way it was, thank you very much.

Then why do I feel as though I need to remind myself?

"The babe is due in August," Driscoll said, "but lately Amelia has grown quite tired by the end of the day, so I don't want her working—not even on the books." He looked over at his brother. "I will find a way to maintain the ledgers and continue to run the club."

"You have Keniel."

"I do, and he is a tremendous help, but we seem to have grown within the past month, which is good, but puts a strain on everyone."

"What about Hunt?"

Driscoll shrugged. "He tries to make it, but with his duties at Parliament, his own young child and Diana increasing once again, he is only able to assist occasionally."

Dante nodded. "Our assignment doesn't fill every evening— hence my presence here tonight. I can certainly come on those off nights."

Lydia tapped Dante on his hand. "Um. I have an idea."

He looked suspicious. "What?"

She took a deep breath, already expecting rejection. "I don't have the same aptitude with numbers as I do with languages, but I showed quite well in my maths classes in the boarding school I attended." When Dante didn't respond, she continued, with hope in her voice. "If we have an evening off and you are working here, why not let me come with you and work on the books?" She looked toward Driscoll. "I assume you would be able to show me what to do?" She didn't want to disparage his wife, but if Amelia could do the books, she was certain she could as well.

Driscoll leaned forward. "Would you be willing to do that? We will pay you, of course."

Lydia waved him off. "That is not a consideration. I am more than happy to help out." Excitement built in her at being able to not only help Dante and his brother, but to be part of this environment so strange and previously forbidden to her that she found so exciting.

Dante held up his hand. "Wait a minute. I'm not sure this is a good idea."

"Why not?" Driscoll and Lydia said at the same time.

He remained silent for a minute. "I don't know, actually." He looked over at Lydia. "Why would you want to work when you have an evening off?"

"What else am I to do on those nights, Dante? Attend another ball? Another musicale—God save my ears—or soiree, rout? While I appreciate Sir Phillip offering me an assignment every once in a while, aside from that I have no purpose in life." She sucked in a breath at her own statement.

How pathetic she sounded before these two hard-working brothers. Did she truly feel as though she had no purpose in life? She was raised to become someone's wife. To manage his household, provide his heirs, and then launch said heirs into society, for them to do the same.

She'd decided a few years back that such a life was not for her. She would feel stifled, almost as if there would not be enough air for her to breathe. But as she stated to the Rose brothers just now, the little bit of enjoyment she received from her Home Office assignments hadn't made for a full life.

And she wanted a full life.

* * *

DANTE WAS STILL CONFUSED as to why he immediately blurted out it was not a good idea for Lydia to work at the club. It had been the perfect solution. If they both came to the club on their free nights, it would help his brother out a great deal.

However, while it might help Driscoll, the arrangement would wreak havoc with his own state of mind. Not one to embrace celibacy, he'd been unable to take care of his needs since he first set eyes on Miss Lydia Sanford in Sir Phillip's office.

None of the women he usually enjoyed, nor any of the ones he'd bantered with at the various *ton* events they'd attended, had appealed to him. Even those who he knew were quite skilled in the bedroom had not tempted him. Despite keeping his libido under control while on an assignment, he had still kissed his partner and insinuated he would like to take her to bed. Only his strong power of control made him end things before they had gone too far.

It was obvious to him that Lydia felt the same powerful attraction between them. Would she have stopped *him* if he had not?

Additional nights with them together would certainly challenge his self-control, which had never been a problem before with any other woman. However, for the good of the club and his brother's peace of mind, he had to withdraw any objection.

"In answer to your question, Lydia, there is no reason why you should not help out if that is your wish."

She smiled brightly, her eyes lighting up, and he sucked in a breath. He reminded himself once again to keep her hidden. In the office. Behind a closed door. Maybe arrange for her to sit under the desk for when other—male—employees visited the office. Maybe set up a desk in the bedroom.

No. Bad idea. Bad, bad idea.

Driscoll leaned back in his chair and grinned. "I appreciate your help, Miss Sanford. And it will relieve my wife's mind as well since she is feeling guilty about me not allowing her to work right now."

The minx grinned at him. "Then it is settled. I will come here when we are not working on the assignment and help out!"

Driscoll slapped the table with his hands. "Wonderful." He stood and headed to the door. "If you have time tonight, I can show you the books since Dante is here to help out on the floor."

She nodded. "Yes."

Once Driscoll left, Dante said, "If you change your mind, Driscoll will certainly understand."

"Why would I change my mind? I like the idea of helping out."

Dante pushed back from the table. "Then I guess I should show you to the office."

"And the gaming floor. Even though I said I wanted to see it when it was crowded, I'd still like to see it now. I imagine I will see plenty of the club when I am working here."

"You will see nothing of the club while members are here. I want to make that perfectly clear."

"Goodness."

The thought of Lydia wandering around the club, being ogled by half-drunk men raised his ire to the point he felt the need to punch something. He'd never felt that way about a woman before, in fact he and a friend had shared a woman or two in the past.

This was becoming dangerous to him and his lifestyle.

Right then he made the decision to do whatever it took to finish the assignment. He would not complain about musicales and other events they needed to attend. Get it all wrapped up and back to his normal life.

Then he immediately contradicted himself by cursing the sense of loss at the idea of them parting ways.

They made a stop by the office where Dante pointed to the

stack of ledgers on Driscoll's desk as well as the other desk where Amelia worked when she was in the club.

Lydia walked around the office, her bright eyes inspecting everything from the bad painting hanging over the file cabinet to the small table with a cold teapot sitting there. "This is quite interesting." She turned to him. "My father would be appalled to know I plan to work."

"You do now. For Sir Phillip."

She waved her hand. "Yes. But he allows that because he says since I have the talent to learn all these languages, I should use it in service to my country."

"I agree." After checking his timepiece, he took her by the hand. "The club will open in about fifteen minutes, so if you want a tour of the gaming floor it must be now."

As they walked down the corridor, she said, "Perhaps I can also learn to deal cards like Amelia did and work on the floor."

"No. We've gone over this before, Lydia. Amelia was in a lot of trouble when she came here late one rainy night and climbed through the window to Driscoll's office. The only reason we allowed her to deal on the floor was because she needed to eat and have a place to sleep. She refused an offer of help and insisted on working for her keep."

"She sounds like someone I would like."

Dante studied her for a minute. "Yes. I believe you would."

"I'd like to meet her."

He cringed at the idea of Amelia, and perhaps even Diana, Hunt's wife, getting to know Lydia. She would fit in with the other women just fine.

Get your mind far away from what you're thinking, Dante.

He could feel the preacher's noose tightening around his neck. "Perhaps one day you will meet her. But now let's go to the gaming floor."

They walked the floor, with him pointing out the various games and how they were played. Then they moved to the perimeter of the room where he waved toward a long table that held various bottles of liquor, and the table on the other side of the room where food would be placed around midnight to keep the players from leaving to eat.

Since gambling was technically illegal, he pointed out to her how they re-arranged the gaming floor to appear as if it were a gentleman's club if they knew a raid was coming. They had friends and members who alerted them when a raid was expected, something the police had to do every once in a while to appease those who felt gambling was a sin.

"It is a wonderful place, Dante. You and your brothers have done such a great job." Her praise warmed him, which scared him at the same time.

"Let's get you back upstairs since we open in about five minutes."

"Didn't you say there was a place I could view the room from where no one would see me?"

"Yes. I will show it to you." He took her hand and they walked back upstairs. It was just his luck that they passed Keniel on the way who grinned at them again. "Ah, the unidentified lady."

Dante gritted his teeth. "Miss Lydia Sanford, this is Mr. Keniel Singh, our club manager."

She held out her hand and Keniel had the nerve to kiss the back of it.

"That's enough," Dante growled. When the manager viewed him with a smirk, he added. "Don't you have work to do, Keniel?"

"I do. However, may I learn why this lovely lady is here this evening? Are you our new dealer, Miss Sanford?"

She laughed. Assuming Mr. Singh was not aware of the work the Rose brothers did for the Home Office, she gave an explanation that would not have Dante glowering at her. "No. Mr. Rose and I are friends and he offered to show me his club.

AN INCONVENIENT ARRANGEMENT

Also, with Mr. Driscoll Rose's wife unable to help with the books, I will be doing that for a while."

"Ah. Then we get to see more of you. Splendid."

Dante scowled as Lydia took note of Keniel. He knew what she saw was an attractive man with smooth caramel colored skin, standing tall and proud, his shoulders wide in his well-cut expensive jacket.

They'd hired him for those very reasons. His self-confidence kept the employees in line and the customers happy.

"I just love your accent, Mr. Singh. I am a connoisseur of languages. May I guess you are from Jamaica?"

"Well done, Miss Sanford." His grin revealed bright white teeth.

Dante was getting annoyed at how well the two of them were getting on. "I think it's time we headed upstairs, Miss Sanford."

"Yes." She looked back at Keniel when Dante took her elbow to move her up the stairs. "It was nice meeting you."

Dante threw a snarling glance at Keniel. "Get to work."

This time instead of a chuckle, Keniel burst out laughing. "Yes, Mr. Boss. I shall do that right now."

$\mathcal{L}$ ydia hadn't been so excited about something in a long time. Years of Polite Society, with all its rules and restrictions, along with the numerous, never-ending balls, garden parties and musicales had become so rote that she moved through the events like a mummy. Smiling at the same people, ignoring gossip as much as possible, and dancing with the same men.

Her few assignments with the Home Office broke up the monotony, but they were few. Even though her skill was remarkable, there was not much need for it.

Now, however she was working at a gaming club! Yes, perhaps she was stuck in the office behind a desk working on numbers, but she felt needed.

They made their way up the stairs and Dante walked her back to the office where he pulled one ledger out from the pile and handed it to her. "This is the ledger Driscoll uses to record the take at the end of the night. I see he has slips of paper in here from the dealers that need to be recorded. Perhaps you can start with that, and I'll send him up to go over more of the information with you."

"All right. Then I shall get busy."

Dante hesitated for a minute, then turned on his heel and left.

About two hours later, Dante arrived back at the office just when she was thinking she desperately needed a break. Her eyes were burning from focusing on numbers for so long.

He held his hand out. "Come, I will show you where you can observe the gaming floor."

She hopped up, happy for the break as well as seeing the club in action. He walked her to a glassed-in area where she could observe almost the entire floor.

"We use this to watch the players on occasion. Sometimes to make sure everything is going well in general, other times to watch for cheating or other signs of nefarious behavior."

"THIS IS INCREDIBLE." She leaned her fingertips against the glass and gazed through the window, taking in all the activity. Shouting, cheering, and groaning rose above the general hum of the crowd. Like ants busily working. Except these people were playing. "I never would have thought that players needed to be watched." She turned to him. "What of your employees? It seems to me they handle quite a bit of money. Are they scrutinized as well?"

"We like to think all of our employees are honest and wouldn't cheat us, but there are occasions." He stopped and thought for a minute and shook his head. "We do watch the new employees for a while, but there's only been one time when we had to let an employee go for cheating."

Since he didn't elaborate on what that occasion had been, she dismissed it.

He checked his timepiece. "I have to go back down to the floor. If you want to continue observing, feel free to do so. I also suggest you take a break and avail yourself of some of the food and coffee set up in the dining room down the corridor."

She perked right up. "Certainly. I think that is a wonderful idea."

LYDIA GLANCED at the clock on the wall. She had been working on the books for two more hours since her break. Driscoll had stopped by and showed her a few things about his method. His system was very straightforward and easy for her to follow.

She stood and stretched deciding it was a good time to take a stroll down the corridor and avail herself once more of the clear glass area where she could see the gaming floor.

The amount of activity stunned her. There must have been over a hundred people milling around the floor. She took special note of the women since Dante had told her 'ladies' were not welcomed at the club. There were no more than a handful, but 'twas obvious they were not the sort of women she would see while riding in Hyde Park in the afternoons twirling their parasols.

Like a small child, she pressed her nose against the glass so she could see more of the room. Just as she was about to pull away to look in another direction, she drew in a sharp breath.

She stopped for a minute, then spun around and raced to the end of the corridor and down the stairs. Keniel stood at the bottom of the stairs, apparently just having left the gaming area.

"Is something wrong, Miss Sanford?"

"No. Yes. Well, actually can you get a note to Dante? It's very important."

"Certainly. Is there anything I can do to help?" He studied her with concern.

"No. Thank you anyway. Do you have a paper and pen?" She was anxious to get word to Dante.

Keniel took her by the elbow and walked her through a maze of rooms of various sizes until they reached a small office. "This is my office. Please make yourself comfortable at my desk. You will find paper in the top drawer and the pen on the desk. I will return in a moment."

She hurried to the desk, pulled out the drawer and quickly penned her note. Unable to sit still, she left the office and attempted to find her way back through the room.

Eventually, she ran into Keniel on his return to her. She held the folded missive out to him. "Please see that he gets this immediately."

Keniel bowed. "Of course."

Lydia took a deep breath and returned to the glass area above the gaming floor.

* * *

DANTE PUSHED himself away from the wall where he stood speaking with one of the club members, Lord Hathaway. The man was in his cups as well as light of pockets. He'd spent the last ten minutes trying to convince Dante to extend him more credit. The fool even offered up one of his country homes as collateral.

Although they were in the business to make money, the brothers had made it a policy to refuse anyone who began to offer properties. Other clubs were not so fastidious, but for the Rose brothers it was a matter of honor. They made enough money without beggaring its members and leaving families with no roof over their heads.

Keniel wove his way through the crowd, apparently heading to Dante. The manager had just left to take a well-deserved break, so it was odd to see him returning so quickly.

Dante moved toward him. "Is there a problem?"

Keniel shook his head and held out a piece of paper. "No, sir. Miss Sanford asked that I deliver this to you."

"Thank you." Dante opened the paper.

The Ambassador is here with the same man.

He took a quiet survey of the room. "Thanks, Keniel. You can return to your break."

Dante made his way over to Driscoll. "I need to speak with Miss Sanford for a minute. Keniel's on his break."

Driscoll waved his hand. "Fine. Things are quiet right now."

Dante took the stairs two at a time. Lydia was waiting for him at the top.

"Where are they?"

She took his hand and walked him to the glassed-in area. She pointed. "There. At the *vingt-et-un* table."

"Damn. I never saw him."

"I believe it is much easier to see everything from here."

They both watched the two men converse as they played their hands.

"I need to get down there and hear what they're saying," Lydia said.

Dante shook his head. "No. You cannot go down to the floor. The liquor has been flowing for a while and I don't feel comfortable letting you walk around."

She tapped her fingernail on her lip. "What if I wasn't walking around?"

He leaned one shoulder against the wall. He could see her devious mind working and couldn't wait to hear what came out of her mouth next. "What do you mean?"

"I mean I know how to play *vingt-et-un* quite well."

Dante grinned and crossed his arms over his chest. "What exactly is it you are proposing, Miss Sanford? You might as well say it out loud before I say no."

"Please listen, Dante. I know how to play the game and I could learn rather quickly how to deal the cards. If they choose to converse in another language, I'll understand what they're saying. It's the same as if we were working a ball, or a musicale. They would never assume someone dealing their cards was listening to them. Think of all the information I might glean."

When he hesitated, she continued. "You've had a female dealer on that table before. It would not seem unusual for me to step in."

Dante pressed the heels of his hands against his forehead. The woman made a lot of sense. It would be the perfect set-up to hear what they were saying without having to sneak behind bushes in the dark.

He looked over at Lydia in the black dress that would have all the men at the table drooling over their cards. "Amelia always wore a mask."

She apparently sensed his surrender. "Perfect! My only concern had been the many men down there that I know from various events. If word got back to my father, but with a mask. . ."

His stomach muscles clenched. Now he knew how his brother had felt when he allowed Amelia to work on the gaming room floor. Except Driscoll had already developed a *tendre* for his wife by then.

So why do you think you feel the same way?

"I would like to find out first how long the Ambassador has been there. It is quite possible we might go through all this trouble and he's about to leave."

"Would Keniel know? Since you hadn't known the Ambassador until recently, you had no reason to note if he favored that table, or even if he spends much time here at all."

"I don't know about Keniel, but I'm sure James, who deals at that table most nights would know."

"Can you get a note to him?"

Dante thought for a minute. "Let me speak to James."

When she attempted to follow him down the stairs, he held

up his hand. "Stay up here. I suggest you go to the dining room and have something to eat and drink. If you do take over James's shift, there are still hours to go."

What the hell was he getting himself into? First it was seeing her only on the nights they had events. Then she ended up asking to see the club. Next, she volunteered to take care of the books on their nights off from the Home Office assignment, at a time when Driscoll desperately needed her help. Now she might very well be working as a dealer.

Lydia was a complete surprise from when he first set eyes on her. There was a rebel inside that woman, chomping to break out. And she seemed able to twist everything he said, coming out the winner in all their verbal spars.

Of course, what she suggested made a great deal of sense. Since Amelia had worked at that table, putting Lydia in there was not a complete deviation from what the club had done before.

He wandered over to James's table and indeed the Ambassador and the man they'd seen with him at the Lenard's ball sat in front of the dealer. He slapped the Ambassador on the shoulder, startling him. "Good evening, Ambassador. Are things well?"

The Ambassador offered Dante a tight smile. "Fine, Mr. Rose. Just fine."

"Glad to hear it." He sauntered around the table and spoke into James's ear. "How long has the Ambassador been here?"

James spoke out of the side of his mouth. "About an hour, but he generally plays until the night ends."

Dante nodded. "You will have a replacement in about a half hour. Act like it's normal."

James continued to deal and gave a curt acknowledgement. Dante returned upstairs and found Lydia in the dining room, just finishing up a plate of food.

He pulled out a chair and sat across from her. "James tells

me the Ambassador generally plays at the *vingt-et-un* table until closing."

Lydia nodded and took a sip of tea.

"I have masks in my office that Amelia used when she was working at the table. If I remember correctly, there is a black satin one there that will fit you perfectly."

Dante groaned at the excitement in Lydia's eyes. Was he making a mistake in letting her take over the table? If anyone from the *ton* recognized her, her reputation would be in ruins. And most likely her father would come after him with pistols loaded and an invitation to meet him at dawn with his second.

However, he was quite sure no one expected to see Miss Lydia Sanford, daughter of Viscount Sterling, dealing cards in a gaming club. That, and the mask should keep her identity secret. Hopefully.

They walked together to the office where Dante pulled out a stack of masks.

Lydia fondled the top mask, a blue satin. "Why do you have so many masks here?"

"Once a year we allow ladies into the club. It's a special event, and no gaming is offered. We provide music and food. It gives the ladies a chance to see where their husbands spend some of their time."

"And money." Lydia smirked and picked up the black satin mask. "This is lovely."

Dante continued. "It's a masked event, and since we allow our employees to attend also, we keep a supply of masks as well as gowns on hand."

Lydia looked up at him. "Allowing your employees to attend is well done, Mr. Rose."

"We feel if our employees are treated well, they have the desire to do a better job."

"I agree." She held out the black satin mask. "This is perfect."

She placed it on her face and tied the ribbons at the back of her head.

"This might just work," Dante said, studying her. She was still much too beautiful, especially with that gown, to not attract attention, and possibly comments, but he would be sure one of the men stood near her table to avoid any problems.

"I know you said you knew the game quite well but dealing in a club is a little different. I told James to give us a half hour before you relieve him, so let's go over some rules, and then have you play a few hands."

They spent about twenty minutes with Lydia dealing the cards to him and three mock players. She stumbled a bit in the beginning, but eventually her playing was smooth enough to take over James's spot.

"All right. I think we are ready." He reached out and adjusted her mask.

They made their way downstairs and across the floor. As expected, Lydia received more than her share of looks and comments. Dante gritted his teeth the entire way to James's table and decided he would be the one to watch her work for the rest of the night.

And to think he'd had the nerve to laugh at Driscoll when he'd done the same thing with Amelia.

Dante tapped James on the shoulder, and when he finished the hand, he held his palms up, facing the players, and stepped back. Lydia moved in front of him and nodded at the group of three men and one woman.

He grew a bit uncomfortable when the Ambassador spent too much time studying Lydia. She ignored him and dealt the cards.

"You look familiar, miss, have you worked here before?" he said.

Lydia looked over at the Ambassador and smiled. *"Pardonnez-moi, mais je ne parle pas anglaise."*

He tapped his finger on the table. "Ah. Too bad. I thought you looked familiar, but the woman I know speaks English."

She shrugged and offered him the grin that people used when they had no idea what the speaker was saying.

Well done, Lydia. Now let us see if we get some information.

9

"*I* don't believe this musicale will be so ear-shattering. I've attended prior ones at the Price home. Both Miss Amy and Miss Margaret are quite talented."

It was the night after Lydia had dealt cards at the Rose Room. She still felt the excitement at being in those surroundings and actually working. Father would be aghast, of course, had he found out, but no one had recognized her, and speaking French all evening discouraged most of the conversation that would have made her uncomfortable.

Except for the young man, who she didn't know, whose French was as good as hers. He'd introduced himself as Mr. Peter Manning. She, of course, did not introduce herself, but offered him a pleasant smile.

When he continued to question her identity, Dante strolled up to the table and stood next to Lydia and glared at the young man. It had amazed her that Dante picked up on the fact that she was uncomfortable because he admitted later his French was meager, at best.

After a few minutes and losing two hands, young Mr. Manning departed the table.

Dante viewed her across the carriage as they made their way through London to the Price townhouse. "I truly do not know how you keep your brain so very sharp with all the events you attend. Please understand I am not disparaging *you*, but wondering how you tolerate it since you are so very different from everyone I've met at these gatherings so far."

"Were it not for the fact that I have very little else to do, I would most likely not bother with most events. Some of them I do enjoy because they are entertaining, like the house party we will be attending starting this Friday. However, most events—"

He held up his hand, panic in his face. "Stop. Did you say a house party?"

She grinned at the distasteful face he made. "Yes. Lord and Lady Battenberg's home for a five-day house party. The Ambassador himself told me he will be attending. With all the time we will spend there, I think this is our best opportunity to learn who is passing him information."

Lydia had to admit she was a tad reluctant to attend the party herself. Not that she minded five days away from the city with entertaining activities and large grounds to ride and walk. Her main concern was being under the same roof with Mr. Dante Rose.

She'd been attracted to the blasted man from the time she'd entered Sir Phillip's office. She knew in advance who her partner was to be and what was required. Sir Phillip always made sure she was comfortable with any man he wanted her to work with.

What she'd known of Dante was his reputation as a flirt, rogue, and rake. She might as well throw in libertine, as well. Although he did not move about in Society, his name was well known among its members.

Despite being the late Earl of Huntington's by-blow, he'd been raised right along with his half-brothers. Once she'd heard the tale, she'd oftentimes wondered how Lady Huntington had felt about that.

The man was too good looking for his own good. That and his well-developed expertise with flirtation drew women to him like a dog to a bone.

Before the initial meeting at Sir Phillip's office, she'd assured herself she was more than ready to take on the assignment and have absolutely no reaction to Mr. Rose.

She tried her best to treat him like any other partner, even to the point of arguing with him and slapping him when he kissed her. Nothing worked. The more time they spent together the more she felt herself falling under his spell.

Cursed man.

He was a true flirt, there was no doubt about that. But she'd also found a hard-working, intelligent man under the shell of libertine. He had also been protective of her the night before when the one young lord had begun to annoy her.

She'd tried over and over again to ignore the women—not ladies—who had draped themselves all over him while he worked. He was pleasant and friendly, but she could honestly say he did not seem to encourage any of them.

Once again the idea of an affair with Dante teased her mind. With his reputation there was no doubt he knew how to prevent conception. As far as she knew—and she had asked around when she had first learned about the assignment with him—he had no by-blows himself.

The most distressing thing about their arrangement was the fact that she had also begun to think in terms of husband, marriage and children. For someone who'd been so adamant against the wedded state, it was a chilling thought. Her biggest concern had been being under a husband's control.

What she'd seen so far with Dante, either her negotiation skills were better than she'd known, or he respected her enough to listen to what she had to say and allow her to do things of which he might not approve.

Her ruminations were interrupted by the carriage slowing down. Dante had apparently been lost in thought, also, since he drew his eyes away from the window where he watched the lights of London pass them by and smiled at her.

Oh, dear. His smile had her insides turning to mush.

He had the audacity to wink. "Are you ready?"

Attempting to calm her now racing heart, she took a deep breath. "Yes. I am."

She gathered her shawl and reticule and moved forward on the seat. Dante stepped out and turned to assist her. His touch was strong, warm, and did not help her racing heart.

They made their way up the steps to the front door that was held open by a butler. "Good evening, Mr. Rose, Miss Sanford."

Lydia was impressed that the butler had recognized them. It appeared their pretend courtship was becoming known.

They followed a footman upstairs and down a corridor to a room filled with other guests, gathered into small groups, chatting away.

Since they would not be announced as they would have been at a ball, they entered the room. And were immediately surrounded by women.

* * *

DANTE HAD SPENT the entire carriage ride dwelling on the upcoming house party. Five days! That meant five nights, also. Five nights when he would be in a bed in the same house where Lydia was in a bed.

Hopefully, the men would be a distance from the women. Although he'd never attended a respectable house party—he grinned—from what he'd heard there was a great deal of room switching at the Upper Crust events.

Much to his chagrin and annoyance they'd barely stepped over their host for the evening's threshold when several women walked in their direction and immediately surrounded him. Aside from his growing feelings for Lydia—not completely admitted just yet—it was rather bad manners for women to step up to him, edging aside the woman with whom he'd entered the room.

He pulled Lydia closer to his body. "Good evening, ladies. I assume you all know Miss Sanford?"

"Yes. Of course. She has been around for years." Lady Emmaline offered a smug smile in Lydia's direction.

"That is true, my lady. And the reason you know that is because you have been around for years, as well." Lydia's smile was friendlier, but still her words cut.

Dante had to forced down the laughter. He turned to Lydia. "Shall we find our seats."

"Dante, I would love if you—and Miss Sanford—would join us." She waved at another young lady seated in a group of chairs tucked away in a corner.

"Thank you so much, Miss Thompson, but I believe Miss Sanford prefers to stay closer to the music." He glanced down at Lydia who seemed to be suppressing a laugh herself.

"Yes. I do prefer closer." Lydia turned to the three women remaining. "I've heard the Misses Price perform before. They are very good."

Dante nodded and moved Lydia way from the startled looks on the women's faces. "Once the Ambassador arrives, we will probably have to switch seats anyway, and I didn't want to be confined in the corner."

She looked up at him. "Is that the only reason you declined her invitation?"

Bloody hell. The woman was still fixated on the attention he drew wherever they went. What was he to say, *yes, that is the reason?* Or admit he had become tired of all the innuendoes and open invitations he'd been receiving? Perhaps the most startling fact was that he'd had no intimate contact with a woman since he'd met Lydia.

Truth be known, this foray into the Beau Monde had him thinking hard about his life up until now. He'd always enjoyed a fondness for women, loved his single state and reveled in his work at the club, watching the business grow with his and his brothers' hard work.

Lately he'd been feeling a bit uneasy about it all. Perhaps it was the women swarming him at every event, or the look of annoyance and in some cases, hurt, on Lydia's face when he bantered with the ladies.

He knew in his heart he owed her nothing. They were partners, doing a job for the Home Office. Once the assignment ended, most likely they would never again cross paths since he had no intention of ever stepping foot into a *ton* ballroom or other event for the rest of his life. Yet never seeing Lydia again did not sit as well with him as it would have weeks ago.

"I suggest instead of taking a seat, we stroll the room and watch for the Ambassador to arrive," Lydia offered.

They kept their heads together, speaking nonsense, just to avoid anyone interrupting them so they could watch the door for the Ambassador.

About five minutes before the musicale was to begin, the man entered, again accompanied by the same companion.

Lydia sighed. "I don't think the man with the Ambassador is our contact. They spend too much time together speaking of Germany and what they miss of the place. I'm beginning to think they are merely friends."

Dante nodded. "I believe you are correct. We must focus on who else he speaks with. He might not be spending a great deal of time with his contact, just enough to get what information he needs."

"I think the house party is our best opportunity." Lydia

looked up at him as they passed the French doors off the music room. "How do you feel about being stuck in the country with members of Polite Society for five days?"

He patted her hand and looked forward as they continued to stroll. "It is not something I would ever do on my own. I've passed up numerous invitations to house parties over the years." He slid his eyes in her direction briefly. "The only ones I have attended were not for ladies."

To his amazement, Lydia blushed. "Oh. I think I know what you mean."

After a few steps, she said, "I believe it's time to take our seats."

Since the Ambassador had finally settled himself in the second row, Lydia and Dante immediately took the seats behind them. The men exchanged a few words in German that Lydia said were merely comments on the room.

Growing frustrated at the lack of progress, Dante barely listened to the two girls who played the pianoforte and the violin. Both were not particularly inspiring, but certainly competent. To his dismay, the Ambassador and his friend left during the brief intermission.

Since Dante and Lydia had become involved in a conversation with Lord Beauchamp and his daughter, they were unable to leave before Mrs. Price called everyone back to their seats.

The second half was the same as the first. Same girls. Same instruments, except a girl who was introduced as their cousin, sang. Again, skilled but not necessarily talented.

As soon as the applause died down, Dante stood and reached out for Lydia. "Are you ready to depart?"

He'd checked his timepiece and decided he had enough time to visit the club for a few hours.

"Are you going to the club?" Lydia asked.

"Yes."

She nodded. "Fine. I will go with you. I'm not tired and I can do some more work on the books."

It would be rude of him to tell her no, but his self-control was slipping. The gown she wore was not as revealing as the one she wore the night before, but still outlined her curves quite well. And a whiff of her now familiar scent was driving him crazy.

They settled in his carriage, and he told himself numerous times he would ignore her, and then after they arrived, he'd let her settle in the office upstairs in the club and he would wander the floor. Distance was a good thing given his frame of mind.

Within seconds, his arm having a mind of its own, he reached across the space, pulled her onto his lap and devoured her mouth like a man who hadn't eaten in days. She must have been in the same frame of mind because she kissed him back with identical fervor.

He tugged her shawl down her arms and cupped her jaw, moving her head back and forth to gain the best position to take the kiss deeper. Lydia gripped his shoulders and moaned when he pulled his mouth away.

He scattered kisses along her jawline and down to the tops of her breasts. Warm, soft, scented skin. Plush. He reached into her neckline and ran his index finger over her nipple. She sucked in a breath and squeezed his arms. "Yes. Do that again."

Aware that the ride to the club was not that long, he shifted her so she was lying on the seat. He covered her with his body and pushed the top of her gown down, revealing her exquisite breasts in the pale moonlight. He suckled. Hard. She gripped his hair, pulling almost to the point of pain.

The carriage stopped. He looked down at her. Swollen lips. Messed hair. The top of her gown almost to her waist. He heard the driver jump down and immediately Dante sat up and opened the door, his body blocking Lydia. "I have this, John. You can return to your seat."

Being a good servant, the man merely nodded. Dante turned back to Lydia and pulled her up. He yanked the top of her gown up and stared at her. She looked well kissed and a bit on the confused side. "Let us wait a minute."

Lydia nodded and licked her lips. He groaned. Waiting was not a good idea either. Dante opened the door and stepped out, holding his hand out for Lydia.

Once they made it to the back door of the club, he placed his hands on her shoulders and turned her toward him. "There is a washing room on the same floor as the office. About three doors past the dining room. You might want to fix your hair."

"Yes. Indeed. That is what I need to do." She seemed much too cooperative for Lydia, so she must have been more than a little affected by their encounter in the carriage.

He walked her upstairs, down the corridor to the washing room. "I will see you when the club closes."

She nodded and he kissed her briefly on the forehead and made a quick exit.

This upcoming house party would be a disaster.

10

*L*ydia leaned her head on the back of the smooth leather seat as her carriage began the trek to the Battenberg estate in Hertfordshire. She'd decided for purposes of maintaining her reputation, it would not do for her and Dante to arrive for a five-day party in the same carriage. Although her lady's maid, Alice, was accompanying her, she would not be considered a chaperone. Thank goodness for Lydia's advanced age. She no longer needed one.

However, based on the last time she and Dante had been together she probably needed one more than any other time in her life. The man had the ability to turn her well-honed brain to mush. But then, it should not have surprised her given his reputation, of which she'd been aware before they'd even met.

At least he had avoided her for the rest of the time they were in the club after the musicale and the scandalous carriage ride. He'd also wisely had one of his employees escort her home when the club closed. She hated the disappointment she'd felt.

Having tossed and turned in her bed most of the night in anticipation of today's trip, she was quite drowsy, and soon the book she'd brought with her to read dropped from her lap and landed on the floor as she slipped into a peaceful slumber.

She awoke when the carriage bounced and tossed her to the floor. "Ouch." She climbed back up onto the seat and looked out the window. Alice reached out to pat her hand. "Are you well, Miss Sanford?"

Lydia rubbed her bottom. "Yes. Just a bit sore." She settled back into the seat. "How long have I been asleep?"

"About two hours."

"Goodness. We must be quite close to the Battenberg estate, then." She moved the window curtain aside with her finger and gazed with glee at the rolling green hills. As much as she enjoyed London, it was always nice to breathe the cleaner air of the countryside.

Hopefully when they finally arrive Lady Battenberg would have arranged for a light repast. Not able to eat upon arising, her stomach was reminding her of that fact.

She picked up her book again and resumed reading. Although she and Alice enjoyed a friendly relationship, the girl was very quiet, and it was not at all strange to take a two-hour trip with them not speaking.

Lydia grabbed for the strap alongside her head as the carriage took a right-hand turn. She looked out the window again and in front of them rose a large mansion, sporting various styles of facades and wings in different styles in a mixture of architecture.

Majestic trees rising above the huge home lined the pathway as they moved forward behind two other carriages. Once they rolled to a stop footmen and maids rushed from the house to help the passengers alight.

Lydia took a footman's hand and climbed down the steps. She shook her skirts out and stretched her back muscles. Lady Battenberg hurried up to her, her arms extended. "Miss Sanford, how lovely to see you." She gripped Lydia's hands, then dropped one hand and waved at the two carriages in front of them. "As you can see several guests have arrived at the same time. If you don't mind, I will turn you over to my daughter, Lady Louisa to assist you and your maid."

Lydia nodded. "Of course. It is a pleasure to be here, thank you for including me." She turned to Lady Louisa. "It is nice to see you as well, Lady Louisa."

Lady Battenberg quickly moved to the carriage in front of them.

Lady Louisa linked her arm in Lydia's. "I will show you to your room so you can get settled. When you've refreshed yourself, tea is served on the patio." The girl looked up at the sky. "Unless it rains, then we'll move it into the drawing room."

They chatted amicably as they made their way into the house and up the stairs. The enthusiasm she generally felt for house parties seemed to double. She hated to think it was because Dante would be attending.

Almost as if Lady Louisa read her mind, she said, "I understand from Mother that Mr. Dante Rose is joining us."

Lydia hoped her blush was not visible in the semi-dark corridor. "Yes. I believe he is expected."

The girl leaned in close. "I cannot believe Mother invited him. He has such a reputation, you know."

Actually, Lydia did not know how Dante came to be included. She assumed since he'd told her an invitation had been sent to him, that Sir Phillip had something to do with it. "You mustn't believe everything you hear, Lady Louisa. A man's reputation can be somewhat exaggerated when gossip is passed from one to another."

Lady Louisa opened the door to a bedchamber. "Perhaps you are correct, Miss Sanford. I guess we shall see for ourselves after he arrives."

Apparently, Lady Louisa had not heard the gossip from London that Lydia and Dante had been arriving at events together. However, the girl's comment about when he would arrive answered the question Lydia wanted to know but had not wanted to ask. He had not arrived yet.

"I will leave you to get settled." Lady Louisa left the room; apparently with guests continuing to arrive, her mother kept her quite busy.

"Alice, I think my deep rose gown for tonight's dinner. I'm sure it needs to be pressed."

"Yes, Miss Sanford."

Lydia moved to the dresser where hot water in a pitcher stood alongside a bowl and washing linens. She washed her face and hands and fixed her hair the best she could.

"Would you like me to re-do your hair, Miss?" Alice asked as she shook out Lydia's rose gown.

"No. I think it is fine. Just continue with your work. I assume refreshments will be available for the servants, so you might want to find your way to the kitchen if you are hungry or thirsty."

Alice nodded and continued to examine the gown. Lydia took one last look in the mirror and left the room. A footman stood at the end of the corridor and directed her to the patio.

A gathering of about twenty people mingled there, conversing in small groups and sipping from teacups. Lydia made her way to a table along the balustrade covered with tea, small sandwiches, fruit and cheese. Another smaller table held fruit tarts and petit fours.

She filled her plate and poured a cup of tea. A footman approached her and offered to carry her things to a table. She thanked him and followed the man to a table with two open seats.

Miss Evermore and Mr. James Williams sat side-by-side. They had recently become betrothed. They didn't seem too happy, but Lydia had heard that it was a match arranged by their parents. Such an old-fashioned notion. She smiled to herself imagining the conversation between her and Father should he ever suggest such a thing.

"Felicitations on your engagement," Lydia said.

They both thanked her in such a way that she felt as though she was insulting them. Deciding to move onto more pleasant matters, she said, "I am so looking forward to this party. Have you heard what entertainments have been arranged?"

Miss Evermore finally smiled. "Yes. There will be boats available for the lake, a picnic, a trip into the village, and I believe Lady Louisa also mentioned parlor games and an evening of musical entertainment."

Everything the young lady mentioned was common to house parties. But since Lydia had never been to one at the Battenberg estate, she'd hoped for something different.

"Do you know if the stables will be made available to the guests?" she asked.

Mr. Williams spoke up. "Yes. That was mentioned."

Lydia loved to ride, but there were few places in Town that she could do so. There was always Rotten Row in Hyde Park, but ladies generally rode in carriages there, or strolled. Few rode horses and if they did, it was at such a sedate pace it didn't seem worth her while.

She made plans to visit the stables after tea and see which horse she would like to ride.

A female gasp and murmering caught her attention. "He did come," she heard someone whisper. She didn't have to turn around to know Dante had arrived.

Damn him for being so elusive that everywhere he went he caused a scene. That, combined with his known charm and good looks would again have the women heading in his direction.

"Good afternoon, Miss Sanford." Dante's deep voice rolled over her as he took the seat alongside her, sitting sideways on the chair so he faced her.

She nodded and held out her hand. "Mr. Rose. A pleasure."

To her annoyance, he laughed. Didn't the man know how to behave in Polite Society? Even though they had appeared together at various events, they were not betrothed, so a certain amount of formality must be preserved.

"I agree, Miss Sanford. It is always a pleasure to see you."

Lydia glanced over at Miss Evermore and Mr. Williams who both sat gaping at them. "Mr. Rose, may I present Miss Evermore and her betrothed, Mr. Williams."

Dante nodded. "Williams. Miss Evermore, a pleasure."

The couple nodded and mumbled a greeting.

"I am a bit hungry. Walk with me while I fill my plate," he said, noticing her plate was empty.

They strolled to the table, being stopped by friends and the usual ladies looking for Dante's attention. He was polite to everyone, but kept her arm linked with his as they made their way across the patio.

"The Ambassador's carriage was just arriving as I walked to the front door." Dante let go of her arm and began to fill a plate. "I have high hopes that we will be able to single out his contact here. With five days for them to connect and spend time together, we should be able to finish this assignment."

The disappointment that always overwhelmed her when thinking of their assignment ending felt as though a cloud passed over the sun. She hated to admit it, but she enjoyed Dante's company. He was funny, charming, thoughtful, and kissed like no one she'd ever kissed before.

But then, didn't all the ladies think so? He would most likely return to his rakish ways once they said their goodbyes.

Well, she had a fine, happy life before she ever laid eyes on Mr. Dante Rose, and she would continue to have one after he was gone.

Maybe.

* * *

DANTE FOUND it bit disconcerting that when he stepped onto the patio his eyes quickly sought out Lydia. Like a magnet, he focused immediately on her sitting with another couple.

Before he could be stopped by other guests, he strolled to the table and took the chair next to her. Each time he saw her, it was if he was seeing her for the first time. Lydia was a beautiful woman, but her beauty also shone from within, with intelligence, wit, and courage.

After he'd lost control in the carriage on the way to the club after the musicale, he'd decided to have one of his employees escort her home. That he didn't trust himself alone with her almost amused him. He had never lost control with a woman.

They walked back to the table that Miss Evermore and Mr. Williams had vacated and took their seats. Within seconds Lady Emmaline and Miss Thompson slid into the chairs. "I hear there will be boats available tomorrow afternoon. I hope you don't disappoint me again, Dante. I do love a ride on the lake." Lady Emmaline offered what he was sure she thought was a sultry look. Instead, she looked desperate.

"I doubt very much if you will be disappointed, my lady. There are many gentlemen here who I am sure would be more than happy to take you out in a boat."

She leaned closer, pressing her body next to his. Why the devil did women wear those cloying scents that had his nose tickling as if he needed to sneeze? She pouted, looking rather silly, actually. "But I had hoped you would take me out in the boat."

There seemed to be no reason to deny her, except he would have preferred to row Lydia out onto the lake and maybe find a quiet spot to . . . "Yes, my lady," he rushed out, "I would be happy to row a boat for you."

He glanced guiltily at Lydia, which was ridiculous since

they had no attachment. They'd made it seem so for purposes of being together to work on the assignment.

Then why did he feel as though he was doing something wrong?

Lady Emmaline preened and looked over at Lydia with glee. Women. They could be so pleasurable and at the same time so annoying.

"How lovely, Lady Emmaline. I am sure you will thoroughly enjoy your boat ride. I, on the other hand prefer to ride horses," Lydia said.

Dante took the clue. "Miss Sanford, may I ask that you permit me to escort you on a ride in the morning? From what I understand Lord Battenberg has an impressive stable."

"That would be wonderful. Perhaps when we are finished here, we can take a stroll to the stables and look the animals over."

"An excellent idea."

"Greetings, my lady." The Ambassador's booming voice reached them. Dante turned to see the man speaking with Lady Battenberg by himself. No companion this time. He glanced over at Lydia who raised her brows. Perhaps the companion was to arrive after him.

Or perhaps the companion they'd been watching was not their man at all.

11

"*I* feel rather silly, the way I've been following the Ambassador around. Clearly he must think I've developed a *tendre* for him," Lydia groused as she and Dante walked their horses out of the stable for their early ride.

It was the morning of the third day of the house party. So far they'd learned nothing, except the Ambassador had an eye for the ladies, and enjoyed his food and spirits. Lydia had tried to be circumspect in her observance of the Ambassador, but she feared it was becoming obvious that she was seeking him out.

"I have hopes for today. With all of us traveling to the village to do a bit of sight-seeing and a stop at the local inn for lunch, we might have a better chance of learning something." Dante helped Lydia onto her horse, and then threw his leg over his mount, leading them away from the stable and out into the countryside.

As was their habit, once free of the confines of the immediate property, they raced over the extensive grounds. Lydia loved the freedom of riding in the country. Rarely did she keep her hat on no matter how many pins she used to anchor it to her head. Then the tidy knot at the back of her head came loose and her hair flew behind her like a banner.

Side-by-side they grinned at each other as they flew over the land. They made three jumps in succession and then drew their horses up, with Lydia, Dante and the two horses all gulping for air.

So far the house party had been nothing but a series of frustrations. Lydia had spent the past two days watching Dante try his best to avoid the women looking for a tête-à-tête, while she attempted to sidle up to the Ambassador and hear his conversations without looking obvious. The man had begun to regard her in a strange way and she had the horrible feeling he might show up at her bedchamber door one night in his dressing gown with a bottle of wine in his hand.

To add to her troubles, she'd tried her best to keep her distance from Dante unless they were mingling with other guests. The temptation to encourage the attraction between them had become too strong. By far the best time of the day had been when they were riding. Together, but separate.

She leaned on the pommel and regarded him. "You seem to be enjoying our rides every morning. I thought you were a confirmed Town man."

Dante grinned at her. "True. I have rarely had a reason to spend time in the country. My father's estate, which went to Hunt along with the title, is only a three-hour drive from London, but with managing the club, I never have a chance to visit."

"Is the Rose Room as busy after the Season ends when most peers escape the heat of London and retire to their estates?" Lydia slowly turned her horse to take a slower walk back to the stables.

"It does slow down. That is generally the time Driscoll and I are able to take a few days off. I hadn't thought much about it, but maybe this year I will join Hunt and Diana in the country for a spell." He paused for a moment. "What about you? Do you retire to the country when the Season ends?"

"My father does. Most times I join him, unless I'm visiting friends' homes outside of London." Lydia took a deep breath, enjoying the air. Perhaps she would join her father and trek to the country after the Season ended.

Then she wouldn't see Dante.

Why had that foolish thought entered her brain? She'd known practically nothing about the man before they started this assignment, yet she was concerned about not seeing him once the assignment ended?

She glanced over at him as they made their return to the stables. There was no denying it. Like most of the ladies of London, she had fallen under Mr. Dante Rose's spell.

Curse the man.

THE GUESTS HAD all gathered in front of the estate to await the carriages for the trek into the village. There were three that would carry the ladies to the village, while the men, except for a couple of the older gentlemen, rode their horses.

There was a festive air about the group. A visit to the local village was always the highlight of a house party. That and shuffling between bedchambers once the guests had retired for the night. Lydia couldn't help but wonder how many women Dante had to chase away from his door.

Her stomach knotted. Unless he hadn't chased them away. However, she sniffed, what Dante did at night once they were all retired was certainly no business of hers.

As if thinking of the man conjured him up like a magician, Dante rode his horse over to where she stood with two other ladies. "Good morning, Mr. Rose. I'm so glad you're joining us on a trip to the village." Lady Emmaline actually tittered. Lydia rolled her eyes.

"It's a fine day for a trip." Dante looked up at the bright blue sky with only a few fluffy clouds floating by.

"I agree. It will be lovely to have a nice long stroll before we meet everyone for lunch at the inn," Lady Emmaline said.

Just then a carriage pulled up. Dante tugged on the brim of his hat and smiled. "I will see you ladies in the village."

They watched him ride off, Lady Emmaline sighing. "He is so very handsome. And such a reputation." She shook her head, looking as if she hoped he would use that bad reputation on her.

Lydia hoped she didn't look as silly as the other women as she, too, watched him ride off. His back straight, his muscular thighs grasping the horse's sides. He sat a horse so well, just like everything else he did. Including kissing.

The women climbed into the large, comfortable carriage. Lydia was joined by Miss Evermore, Lady Louisa, Lady Cambridge and her daughter, Miss Susan. The door no sooner closed when Mrs. Martin came hurrying down the path waving her arm. "Wait."

Lydia had to laugh. Mrs. Martin was a sweet woman but seemed to have a hard time keeping herself organized. She climbed into their carriage, out of breath, with her hat askew. "Oh, my. I tried very hard to be on time, but I couldn't find the shoes I wanted to wear with this outfit."

"Mrs. Martin, it would do you well to hire a lady's maid. I can't imagine trying to keep track of all my things without Maisie," Lady Cambridge said.

"I share a lady's maid with my sister, Anne who lives with me. Her name is Marie, but she stayed home with my sister who needs her more than I do." Mrs. Martin turned to Lydia. "My sister is not well. That's why she stayed home." She leaned in close to her ear and whispered. "She likes her spirits."

It was obvious the other ladies tried their best to hear what Mrs. Martin said, but she whispered low enough. Lydia was a bit uncomfortable since whispering while in company was the worst of manners. She sighed and looked out the window, hoping the ride to the village was not long.

Miss Evermore kept the other ladies busy with passing along all the gossip she seemed to know, that no one else did. The time went by with a great deal of 'oh, no' and 'goodness' and 'the poor girl'. All of it said with glee since the women were only too happy to learn something that hopefully their other friends did not know. Gossip was the ladies of the *ton's* favorite pastime.

Perhaps that was another reason Lydia had been feeling a bit lost recently. As if she no longer belonged. Maybe dealing cards at the club that one night had shown her another world, and for a short, exciting period of time, she'd been part of it.

The carriage stopped at the village center where numerous stands had been set up with goods for display. "I wonder if it is like this all the time, or if we are lucky enough to be here on market day," Mrs. Martin asked.

Shops that lined the village green also had wares for sale on tables in front of the stores. Lydia's spirits picked up. "I shall have so much fun going through the vendors."

They all climbed from the carriages, the men having ridden to the stables, arriving ahead of them. They walked back across the green toward the women. Dante walked directly up to her. "Miss Sanford, may I escort you around the green?"

"Yes, thank you." She took his arm and they walked off to the sound of the women behind them whispering. Honestly, 'twas becoming quite annoying. "How do you stand all the attention you get?" She was afraid her words came out quite harsh.

Dante raised his brows. "Now you know why I avoid these events. I like my work, I like the social life I have devised for myself, and I want nothing to do with Polite Society. And given my birth, I am quite sure Polite Society wants nothing to do with me."

"I never did understand that. If you were born on the wrong side of the blanket, why does that disparage you? You had nothing to do with it."

"Ah, you must ask that question of Polite Society one day. But not on my behalf," he added.

They walked up to an older woman standing behind a table full of sweet- smelling soaps. "I believe I'm growing just as weary of the Season as you are," Lydia replied as she picked up one of the soaps and smelled it. Smiling at the woman, she said, "This is wonderful. Can you wrap up four of them for me?"

"All the same scent, my lady, or different ones?"

"Oh, let's be daring today. Wrap up four different ones."

Once she had her soaps in hand, Dante took her by the arm, and they continued to browse the tables. As they strolled away from a woman selling ribbons, Lydia said, "Do you feel as though this house party was a waste of time in finding any information on the Ambassador?"

"Yes." Dante nodded. "I'm beginning to think this entire assignment is a waste of time. The only contact we've seen the Ambassador make that looked in the least bit suspicious was the man who you've determined is merely a friend looking for a comrade to speak about how wonderful their country is compared to England."

Just as he finished his words, the Ambassador walked out of one of the stores along the village green. Dante immediately moved her in the direction of the store. "Let's see what he bought in there."

The small shop was a bakery with wonderful aromas coming from within. Lydia strolled up to the counter and spoke in German, complimenting the woman behind the counter on the lovely shop.

When the woman appeared confused, Dante took over and

asked if she had lemon tarts for sale. When she pointed to a tray of luscious looking tarts of all sorts, Dante asked for two lemon and took out coins from his pocket and paid her.

Once they were outside, Lydia turned to him. "It was a gamble that she knew German, but I thought if she did, that would have increased our chances of her being his contact."

Dante smiled. "I figured that was what you were doing. But these lemon tarts smell wonderful. What say we wander over to the bench there near the water and eat them?" He waved to an area set aside for relaxation. Three stone benches sat in a circle with a huge oak tree in the middle of the arrangement. Not far from the benches was a small stream.

"A fine idea, Mr. Rose. My mouth is watering already in anticipation."

* * *

Dante steered Lydia to the stone bench, and they sat. He unwrapped the tarts and handed one to her.

Lydia inhaled deeply. "They smell divine." She took a bite and closed her eyes and moaned. Dante almost dropped his tart watching her. She looked like a woman in the throes of passion.

"Um, don't do that." His voice was raspy.

She opened her eyes. "Do what?"

He waved his lemon tart at her. "That. What you just did."

"I took a bite of my tart." She looked at him with confusion.

"Never mind. It's my problem, not yours," he mumbled. And it truly was his problem. He had tried to stay as far away from Lydia during the house party that he could without compromising their investigation. He didn't think it was his imagination that Lydia was avoiding him as well. They functioned together quite well in groups, but they both seemed to be avoiding being alone, except for their morning rides.

Damned if he didn't feel an attraction to her so strong that he'd passed up a number of offers to join him in his bedchamber from women who at one time would have had him jumping for joy. The thought of holding any woman except Lydia in his arms left him cold.

The worst part had been the dreams he'd endured since they'd arrived at the house party. If Lydia uncovered looked as good as she did in his dreams he would never want to leave the bed once he got her there.

Except he had no intention of getting her anywhere near his bed. Despite all her talk of independence and sophistication, given her upbringing, she would expect an offer of marriage if they did succumb to their temptation. She might protest that wasn't so, but he knew she would regret it and end the little bit of friendship they had.

As they strolled the area, looking at various goods and products from the street vendors as well as the shops, he tried his best to ignore the scent coming from Lydia and the softness and warmth of her body next to his.

They arrived at the inn where they were all gathering for lunch. The Ambassador waved at them as they entered and patted the seat next to him. "Miss Sanford, please join me. I've saved you a seat."

Lydia looked over at Dante, who noticed there was only room for one. He shrugged and Lydia joined the man. Dante found a seat at the next table with Mr. Williams, Miss Evermore and Mrs. Martin. They all greeted each other and discussed the morning, the places they'd visited and the things they'd bought.

It was apparent from the sound of the Ambassador's voice that he must have headed directly to the inn after leaving the bakery. He was close to being in his cups.

They placed their orders and Dante found himself studying the Ambassador and Lydia. It appeared that Lydia was becoming uncomfortable. The Ambassador leaned toward her and kissed her on the neck. She drew back and shook her head.

Dante stood and glared at the man. He didn't notice. He sat back down as their food arrived but kept his eyes on the activity at the other table. Once again the Ambassador leaned close to Lydia and whispered something in her ear. She shook her head and shifted on the bench. He slung his arm around her shoulders and pulled her against his body.

Lydia elbowed him, but he continued to hold her. Her face was red, and she looked ready to punch him, which was something a lady never did. Especially in public.

Dante had had enough. He stood and marched over to Lydia's table. "Excuse me, Mr. Ambassador, but please refrain from touching Miss Sanford. It is obvious she is not enjoying your attentions."

The Ambassador waved him off, swaying on the bench. "Yes, she is. She's been following me around for the past two days." He looked up at Dante, his eyes bloodshot. "*Geh zuruck zu deinem Tisch.*" He pulled Lydia against him again and Dante reached over, dragged the man off the bench and plastered him a facer. He went down like a bag of rocks. Dante took Lydia's elbow and helped her up. He threw some coins on the table and they left.

"What did he say to me?" he asked as they left the dimness of the inn and stepped into the sunlight.

"Go back to your table," she mumbled as she turned to watch the Ambassador snoring on the floor before the door to the inn closed.

"*I* can't believe you hit the Ambassador." Lydia shook her head as they strolled away from the inn. "Will you be arrested?"

Dante laughed without mirth. "No. He's lucky I only hit him. The man was behaving in an obnoxious way. And he was drunk."

"But still." She shook her head, trying not to find humor in what happened. The Ambassador had, indeed, become annoying. In fact, had there not been other people around she might have found him frightening. "He is the German Ambassador, though. I'm sure he can create some trouble for you."

"Not as much trouble as we plan for him." He smirked. "Now bringing him down has become personal for me."

They took the short walk from the inn to the center of the village. "What about the others? They're still having lunch. In fact, I'm hungry. But I don't suppose we can go back to the inn."

"No. But there are vendors here on the village green who are serving food. Oftentimes it's far superior to a inn." He took her by the hand and led her into the gathering of tables and sellers hawking their wares. A touch that seemed much more intimate than linking their arms.

Every time he touched her, tingles began in her middle. Although she'd been surprised to see Dante punch the Ambassador, and she still wasn't sure there wouldn't be trouble for it, the feeling of protectiveness she'd seen in Dante appealed to something very feminine in her. Something desirous as well. Once again she pondered the idea of an affair. Then she dismissed it out of hand. That would involve a great deal of sneaking around and being well known within the *ton*, she would soon be discovered and ruined.

Ruined for what? If she had no intention of marrying, should she care so very much about her reputation? Yes, the small annoying voice answered. It would destroy her father.

Shifting her attention from the warm strong hand that held hers to the area where he led her, it appeared that those selling food were gathered in one place, which made it easy to find whatever they wanted with delicious scents in the air. All they had to do was follow their noses.

Lydia's eyes lit up. "Oh, meat pasties. I love those. Cook refused to make them, she said they were uncivilized."

Dante huffed. "If I was paying someone to cook for me, they would cook exactly what I wanted or find themselves out on the pavement."

Lydia watched his face as he spoke. Despite his rearing and connection to a very imposing peer, there was something fearsome in Dante's demeanor. But then again pummeling the Ambassador in front of witnesses was certainly not a typical way for a house guest to behave. "Do you think Lord Battenberg will ask you to leave?"

Dante stopped in front of a stand where the aroma of meat pasties had her mouth watering. "If he does, which I doubt, you are leaving with me, and damn the investigation. I'm not leaving you here in the Ambassador's nefarious clutches."

Once again that feeling of being protected and cared for arose. Which was silly since Dante would probably act the same for any woman.

The young woman behind the table with a toddler clinging to her skirts handed them two steaming meat pasties. This time instead of finding the stone bench again, they strolled along, nibbling on their food. Lydia felt a bit odd at first. Never had she eaten outdoors while strolling along. 'Twas just not done. Not in her world, anyway. But Dante's world was much more interesting. And fun.

She licked her fingers—Father would be appalled—and smiled. Life was truly fascinating when one let go of the rules and regulations. She had to admit, however, being away from anyone who knew her granted her a certain amount of freedom. The ladies of the *ton* were always watching and judging.

"'Tis time for liquid." Dante flashed his famous suggestive smile. "Since we have flaunted propriety so far, perhaps a mug of ale as we stroll along would be just the thing."

"Yes! I would love an ale. And you are correct, I have been flaunting propriety all day." She surprised herself by twirling in a circle. "And I love it!"

Dante grabbed her arm and pulled her close to avoid crashing into an older couple strolling along. "Easy, love. You don't want to call too much attention to yourself."

"I agree. However, you have no idea how different your life is." She gave some thought to the words she was about to say but said them anyway. "I...um, believe I prefer your life to mine; at least the life I've been living." She looked up at him, mortified to feel the tears gathering in her eyes. She blinked rapidly to keep them from falling.

Dante pulled her closer to his body and despite being outside in public, kissed her on the top of her head. "You have the power to change anything you want about your life."

She grimaced. "No, that is not true, and what if my wishes

are not available?" Would he guess she meant him? She'd come to believe that her life could be so much more fulfilling if she had a purpose, like Dante did. He ran a club, he had freedom—which of course, came from him being a man. But there had to be something for her to add to her life that would take away the recent sense of uselessness that had troubled her.

The days, months, and unfortunately the years, had gone by quickly. She'd gone from a hopeful debutante to a jaded spinster. No man had captured her heart. Truth be known, no man had appealed to her enough to even get close enough to capture her heart.

Until now. Why did she start to believe in a happily ever after with a man who had stated loud and clear that he had no intention of ever marrying? Why develop a *tendre* for a man who was a known rake and rogue, who could never be satisfied with one woman?

Apparently sensing her mood, he patted her hand. "No worries today, sweeting. We've had our excitement for the day. While we await the consequences of my very satisfactory actions, I say we enjoy this day and not think of the future."

Sweeting? That was the second time he referred to her in an intimate way. Of course, he most likely spoke that way to every woman he spent time with. She should not make something of nothing.

As he said. Enjoy the day and not think of the future.

* * *

DANTE ATTEMPTED UNSUCCESSFULLY to forget the look on Lydia's face when she spoke about the uselessness of her life and how she much preferred his. The tears threatening to slide down her beautiful cheeks had torn him up. Truth be known, he'd never given much thought to a woman's life.

Outside of the bedroom, that is. He'd always made sure his

bed partners were well satisfied once they left him and the few times he'd employed a mistress, he was diligent in making sure they were happy with the jewelry and other things he left them with upon his departure. Many a tear could be dried by an expensive bracelet or necklace.

Knowing Lydia had been an eye-opener for him. He'd always avoided Polite Society since he hated the restrictions himself. He never imagined how much more difficult it was for a woman. The ones he'd bedded from the Upper Crust had been widows with no concerns about their reputations as long as they were discreet.

He was fully aware of what Lydia had meant when she said that perhaps the life she wanted was not available to her. At one time he would have found it quite easy to dismiss her comment, since he was *not* available.

Was that still true? If the allure between them was the cause of how much he enjoyed Lydia and sought out her company even when it wasn't part of the investigation, then perhaps his adamant insistence on never attaching himself to one woman was in danger.

Pushing the disturbing thought to the back of his mind, he purchased two large cold mugs of ale and handed one to her, the foam dripping over the side. She looked up at him while she licked the drippings and all his blood traveled south. He shook his head and grasping her hand, continued their stroll.

By the time they finished their drinks and returned the mugs to the vendor, the house party guests were beginning to leave the inn and assemble in the village square. He noticed that the carriages had re-appeared and the men began the trek to the stables to retrieve their horses.

The Ambassador was with the group, but it was obvious he was having trouble walking since he was flanked by Mr. Williams and Lord Monroe. They brought him to one of the carriages, and Dante steered Lydia to another one. "I don't want you near him. And you are not to follow him around anymore. We will find another way to bring this cursed assignment to an end."

Lydia reared back. "I don't believe I need you to tell me what to do and what not to do. I can certainly take care of myself."

His raised brows belied her statement. When she'd been in the company of the others she'd been annoyed at the Ambassador's behavior, but certainly not in true danger. However, with her following the man about, trying to hear his conversations, she had put ideas into the Ambassador's head. Ideas that Dante was not at all pleased about.

"I apologize. I don't wish to tell you what to do, but I'm insisting that you should discontinue following the Ambassador trying to hear his conversations. I'm thinking this party is not the best place to watch him. Firstly, if he were going to make contact with one of the guests—"

"—or staff."

He nodded. "We would have seen it by now. No one new is expected, so I doubt the next couple of days will garner any worthwhile information."

"Are you coming, Miss Sanford?" Mrs. Martin leaned out of the carriage door. "We are about to leave."

"Yes." Lydia turned to Dante. "We can continue this later." She climbed into the carriage and closed the door.

Dante made his way to the stable to retrieve the horse he'd ridden to the village.

"That was some wallop you gave the Ambassador back there." Mr. Williams nodded at the departing carriages. "I had to agree with you, though. If he tried that with Miss Evermore I am certain I would have done the same."

"Me as well," Lord Monroe said. "He had definitely been behaving in a most ungentlemanly manner and quite an insult to Miss Sanford."

Dante shook his head and swung his leg over the horse. "The man's a bloody ass." He was unable to share with the others just how much of an ass the man was, but through his actions, the Ambassador apparently had not made a good impression on the men.

THE END of the house party had arrived. Dante had managed to avoid tapping on Lydia's bedchamber door the entire time, of which he was both proud and annoyed. His desire for her, if anything, had increased. Which, in turn, had made it quite easy to continue turning down the insinuations and blatant offers from other women to join him in his bedchamber.

The Ambassador had departed the party the night of the inn fiasco. Dante had been in favor of him and Lydia leaving as well, but it would raise questions they didn't wish to encourage. Much to his annoyance they were trapped. Damn if he could figure out why these *ton* house parties were so popular.

This evening would be the ball that traditionally ended all house parties. Gentry from the surrounding area would join the house guests. He was more than ready to depart and get back to London. As much as he'd enjoyed the rides in the morning with Lydia, the rest of the time, especially with the Ambassador gone, had truly been a waste of time.

His opinion of the frivolous life of the *ton* had been reinforced by this foray into Polite Society. Since he'd always worked for his living—once he'd given up the allowance Hunt had set up for him and Driscoll—he found nothing but contempt for those who depended on inheritances, or worse yet, marrying rich American heiresses to keep their pockets full.

"You look absolutely stunning," Dante said as he took Lydia's hand and kissed it before linking her arm with his and steering them toward the ballroom.

Stunning hadn't even covered it sufficiently. Her peach satin gown with black embroidery on the hem and edge of the sleeves fit her to perfection. The neckline was so enticing, showcasing her beautiful breasts, that he reluctantly quelled the desire to hustle her back up the stairs to his bedchamber and forget all the congratulations he'd been giving himself for not having dragged her to his bed before now.

Since he and Lydia had arrived in separate vehicles, early the next morning they would return that way, which given his state of mind just being near her, was the best idea he'd ever had. All he had to do was get through this blasted ball and then he could return to his normal life and stop being so tempted by his partner.

All the men of the party, and even a few of the gentry made their way to Lydia to request dances. Luckily Dante had anticipated that and had already filled in a quadrille and a waltz just as they'd entered the ballroom. It would not sit well with him to watch her dance with other men, but since he had no claim on her, he said nothing.

In order to keep his mind from thinking about that, he'd signed the dance cards of other ladies. Everyone seemed to be in a jovial mood except him. He glanced at Lydia, speaking with Lord and Lady Battenberg. His partner had shown more enthusiasm at eating a meat pasty and drinking ale in public than she did at this ball.

Upon returning from the trek to the village, Lord Battenberg had taken him aside and while he'd not actually congratulated Dante for planting a facer on the Ambassador, he did remark that the man had it coming to him. Dante got the impression that Lord Battenberg was not overly fond of the Ambassador.

The musicians had been testing their instruments, and then it all came together, and they began the first dance of the evening. The waltz he and Lydia were to share.

As was the usual procedure, Lord and Lady Battenberg began the dance alone, and then were soon joined by other couples. Dante swung Lydia into his arms, and everything seemed right with his world.

Hell and damnation he was in trouble!

13

*D*ante took the steps two at a time up to Viscount
Sterling's townhouse. He rapped on the door and it
was quickly opened by the butler. "Good morning, Mr. Rose.
Miss Sanford is expecting you in the drawing room. If you will
follow me."

Two days had passed since the end of the house party.
Dante had spent that time working at the club so Driscoll
could take a break and spend time with his wife. Lydia had
worked on the books both nights and it had been no surprise
to Dante that she did the work quickly, clearly, and efficiently.

Just another thing to admire about the woman.

Lydia might have been expecting him, but it was Lord Sterling who greeted him, with his daughter nowhere in sight. The
man stood as Dante entered and held out is hand. "Good
morning, Mr. Rose. So nice to see you."

The older man had retained most of his hair, although it
had turned silver over the years. He was fit for his age, which
Dante guessed to be somewhere in his fifties.

"Please have a seat. My daughter will be down shortly."

That gave him pause. It sounded as if Sterling had met him

here instead of Lydia for a reason. Dante fidgeted in his seat and ran his finger around the inside of his necktie.

He knew Sterling from the times the man had visited the club. He was a cautious player, never losing more than fifty pounds per visit. He was well liked by the club's staff and the other club members.

"Would you care for a drink?" Sterling asked.

"No. Thank you, but 'tis a bit early for me."

"Coffee?"

It seemed Lydia's father was planning on making this an actual visit. Dante discreetly checked his timepiece. Their meeting with Sir Phillip was in half an hour. It was about a twenty-minute ride to the man's residence.

Dante had received the summons from the Home Office contact yesterday afternoon. Once Lydia had arrived later that evening to work on the books, he'd showed it to her.

My Dear Mr. Rose,

I would like to see you and Miss Sanford in my office at eleven tomorrow morning. We must discuss the case.

Sir Phillip DuBois-Gifford

Lydia had returned the note to him. "I wonder what this is about?"

Dante had shrugged and stuck the note into his pocket. "We will find out soon enough."

He brought his mind back to the present. "No, thank you, my lord. Miss Sanford and I are expected at a meeting. I'm afraid I must decline your offer of coffee."

Sterling rubbed his hands together. "Yes. The meeting. Lydia told me about it." He leaned back in his chair and crossed one leg over the other. "How goes the investigation?"

Dante was surprised that the man seemed familiar with their assignment. However, always cautious, Dante merely said, "Not as well as we had anticipated, but I'm hoping we will finish up soon."

Sterling nodded. "Yes. Some of these things can be quite trying." Out of nowhere the man said, "I understand you punched the Ambassador in the nose for getting out of hand with my daughter."

Well, then.

The man apparently knew more than Dante had thought. "Yes, my lord. I was uncomfortable with the Ambassador's actions and when Lydia—er, Miss Sanford—attempted to stop him and he refused, I believe I did what any man would do."

He nodded again. "Indeed. Thank you for seeing to my daughter, Mr. Rose."

"I don't wish to seem rude, my lord, but Miss Sanford and I need to leave shortly if we are to make our meeting on time."

"Yes, yes." Lord Sterling slapped his thighs and stood. "I will send for her." He stuck out his hand and shook it once more. "Nice to see you, lad."

Lad? He'd not been a lad for ages.

With that he left the room and within minutes Lydia entered. "I'm ready."

Dante pushed the unusual meeting with Sterling aside and escorted Lydia out the door and down the steps to his awaiting carriage.

Once they were settled and Dante tapped on the ceiling to alert his driver that they were settled and ready to leave, Lydia said, "What did my father want with you?"

Dante shrugged. "I have no idea."

"He asked me to wait in my bedchamber until he sent for me because he wanted to have a word with you."

He smiled. "That was about all we had. A word. He offered me a drink, and then coffee and asked about the investigation. I assume someone told him about the altercation with the Ambassador at the inn."

Lydia shook her head. "I didn't tell him. I guess the word has spread around Polite Society." She looked out the window at the passing stores as they left the better part of London to the place where Sir Phillip had an office. Or a residence. Dante never did figure out if the man lived there or not. It was certainly not in the best neighborhood.

She cleared her throat. "Now don't panic, but I'm afraid my father has designs on you." She avoided his eyes, which was very unlike the Lydia he knew.

"While I am flattered, I'm afraid I don't lean in that direction." He grinned, but just to be certain he understood what she said, he asked, "What sort of designs?"

She sighed and finally looked at him. "He has never given up on me marrying. Although he encourages my work with the Home Office, he still imagines me married with children clinging to my skirts."

"Perhaps he wants grandchildren." The picture that popped into his mind of Lydia's body swollen with his child, caused him to almost smile. Almost. "You are an only child."

"It's not humorous, I'm afraid. I thought he had given up on that the last year or so." She looked back out the window again. "Perhaps us working together had not been a good idea."

Truthfully, Dante had no idea how to respond to that. Yes, he found Lydia attractive, smart, and easy to talk with. She was generous with her time, stepping in to help at the club, and every one of the staff had nothing but good things to say about the daughter of a viscount working in a gaming business.

Did he still want to take her to bed? Absolutely. Was he having a hard time keeping his hands off her? Yes. Did he want to take the chance of moving things further along, knowing that those actions on his part might very well lead to something he'd sworn all his adult life to avoid?

Ah. There was the crux. He had no answer to that one.

* * *

LYDIA HAD GONE through a difficult interview with her father earlier that morning. Father had heard about the house party and how Dante had come to her defense and punched the Ambassador.

Even though Dante rarely attended *ton* events, attacking the Ambassador in public at a house party—a highly daunting occurrence—Lydia was not surprised that Father had known about it.

What had been even more alarming was Father's questions about Dante, his brothers, his club, and how long the assignment would last. Then when he asked to speak with her partner before they set off for Sir Phillip's home, she grew quite nervous.

Would her father demand Dante apologize to the Ambassador? Or worse yet, somehow tie Lydia's reputation into the entire matter and pressure Dante to rescue her from ruin? Everyone knew what the rescue would involve.

Since Dante hadn't looked bruised when she arrived in the drawing room, they apparently hadn't come to fisticuffs. Neither had Father declared a wedding was to take place posthaste which most likely would have given Dante a pallid look.

"Don't let that disturb you, Lydia. Your father and I had a nice chat. Remember I know him from the club." He pointed his finger at her. "Which is another reason for you to stay hidden in the office when working on the books. You might have been able to fool other club members with your mask the night you dealt at the *vingt-et-un* table, but I'm sure your father would recognize you in a flash."

She relaxed a bit knowing their conversation had been friendly. But she didn't believe for one minute that Father wasn't sizing up Dante as a potential son-in-law.

Dante leaned back on the squab and regarded her. "I don't think we need to concern ourselves about working together. I feel there is a good chance Sir Phillip is not happy with our non-progress."

Lydia sighed. "I believe you are right. Do you think we might be removed from the assignment?" What if Sir Phillip did remove them from the investigation? Dante would go back to his normal life, and with him back at the club, there would be no reason for her to continue with the books since Driscoll would resume the job. Just as everything had been before she'd come into his life. Chances are she would never see him again.

Now there was a depressing thought. They rode in silence for the rest of the time as she dwelled on how to keep Dante in her life. The only two ways she knew were to become his mistress or his wife.

She would have a hard time with the first one since she knew so many people discretion was unlikely. Dante was most adamant about the second one.

Sir Phillip answered the door himself at their knock. "Good morning, Miss Sanford, Mr. Rose. Please step into my office."

The man seemed rather cheerful, so perhaps he wasn't planning on removing them from their assignment.

Once they all settled into chairs, with Sir Phillip behind his large, very cluttered desk, and Lydia and Dante sitting in the chairs in front of the desk, Sir Phillip cleared his throat. "Thank you for coming so quickly." He leaned his forearms on the desk and studied them. "Where are we in this investigation?"

Dante sat up straighter. "Not far, I'm afraid, sir."

Sir Phillip drilled him with his eyes. "Perhaps giving the Ambassador a bloody nose at an inn during a house party set you back a few steps?"

Lydia tried not to smile at Dante's uneasiness.

"'Tis hard to say, Sir Phillip since I don't believe we were very far along before that incident happened."

"But it might keep the Ambassador far from you. How do

you propose to gather information from him if the man is concerned that you might attack him again?"

Dante glared at the man. "If he would keep his hands off—" Lydia nudged him.

He took a deep breath. "I have no idea what you've heard, sir, but I did not attack the man. He was behaving in a grossly improper way toward Miss Sanford. She had asked him to leave her alone, but the snake was drunk and refused to listen to her. I did what I had to do." He tugged on the cuffs of his jacket.

Lydia felt the color rise to her cheeks when Sir Phillip swung his head in her direction and stared. "And what about you, Miss Sanford. Do you feel it was necessary for Mr. Rose to defend you in such a manner?"

She hesitated and could feel Dante's eyes boring into her. "Yes, I do. No other man at the table did anything except stare at the Ambassador. I asked him more than once to leave me be. I even elbowed him, but he would not stop."

Seeming satisfied with their explanations, Sir Phillip nodded and continued. "I still think you two are the best chance of us uncovering the individual who is passing along secrets to the Ambassador. However," he nodded at Dante, "while you are defending Miss Sanford's reputation," he swung his attention to her, "and you are defending his actions, Miss Sanford, the Crown's secrets are leaking from a high echelon source."

They both jumped when Sir Phillip slapped his hand on the desk. "We need that information!" He stood, dismissing them.

"We will not fail at this, Sir Phillip." Dante helped Lydia up from the chair and they made their way out of the office, down the corridor to the door, then down the steps to the awaiting carriage.

Once they settled in, Dante said, "That was not as bad as I had imagined. However, I believe a respite to a tea shop so we can go over our movements so far, and what we need to do in the future, is in order."

Lydia nodded. "I agree. I've never failed at an assignment before, and do not intend to do so now."

"Me, neither. Nothing would please me more than seeing the Ambassador shipped back to Germany. And whoever is passing secrets sitting in prison."

They stopped at the small tea shop they'd visited before. Once they'd ordered their tea, Lydia said, "I think a visit to the Embassy is in order." She hesitated, watching for Dante's response. "By me. Alone."

"No." He shook his head. "Absolutely not." He tapped his finger on the table in a cadence.

Lydia covered his hand with hers. "Listen to me. If I go and apologize for what you did—" She held up her hand as Dante started to object. "I can get back into the Ambassador's good graces."

"That is precisely where I do not want you to be."

Lydia shook her head. "Let me finish. If the Ambassador thinks I disapproved of what you did, I might regain my position to his inner circle again."

"No. That is not going to happen."

She sighed, then looked up at the waiter who brought their tea and laid it all out in front of them. "Thank you."

As she poured their tea, she continued. "You are with me every time I am near the Ambassador, so nothing will happen."

He accepted the cup of tea from her. "And what about a visit to his office? Didn't you just say you wanted to go alone?"

"Yes. But for heaven's sake, it's an Embassy. There are people all over the place."

Dante shook his head. "I still don't like it."

"We must begin to move forward with this. Sir Phillip is losing patience and I agree with him. As he reminded us, while we are working on this, secrets—most likely vital ones—are being passed along to a foreign country."

They both remained silent as they drank tea and nibbled on small sandwiches and biscuits. Finally, Dante said, "I will allow this. On one condition."

Lydia huffed. "I don't need your permission, Mr. Rose. This is a good strategic move, and you know it."

"That is why I am allowing it."

"Don't. Say. That. Word. Again," she growled.

He had the nerve to grin. "I apologize, Miss Sanford. I will re-phrase that. I will have no objection to your plan providing I accompany you and wait in the carriage."

Lydia sat back and thought about it. She doubted very much if she would be in any sort of danger visiting the Ambassador at the Embassy. However, since this would be their first encounter since the debacle at the inn, it might not be a bad idea to have Dante nearby.

"Very well, then. When I arrive home I will pen a note to the Ambassador, asking for an appointment."

"And the minute you receive an answer, you will notify me."

She gritted her teeth. He was so stubborn. "Yes. I will notify you."

Dante raised a finger. "Also, you will only accept an appointment with him during his normal business hours. No after-hours visits."

"Of course. I am not foolish."

Lydia finished the last of her tea and placed the cup in the saucer. After patting her mouth with a napkin, she said, "All right, so why don't we talk about something more pleasant."

Dante raised his brows. "Such as?"

"Such as when can I deal cards again at the Rose Room?"

$\mathcal{L}$ydia took a deep breath as Dante's carriage came to a stop in front of the German Embassy. She had a ten o'clock appointment with the Ambassador. He'd returned her missive for a meeting immediately after receiving it. That was a good sign, she hoped.

Dante stepped out of the carriage and reached for her hand. "Assignment or no, if he gets out of hand, I want you to leave immediately."

Lydia shook her skirts out and adjusted her hat. "I've told you before, with it being only ten o'clock, the embassy is full of people working. I doubt he can do anything nefarious."

Dante snorted. "I don't trust the man." He shook a finger at her. "And neither should you. He's already tried once to take advantage of you, and he is suspected of passing Crown secrets. I hardly consider him an upstanding individual."

She patted him on the cheek. "I will be fine."

He crossed his arms over his chest and glared at her as she turned and walked into the Embassy.

"Miss Sanford to see the Ambassador," she said when she walked up to the man seated behind the desk. He was a young man, stocky, and pleasant. He bowed. "Certainly." He waved to a comfortable looking chair against the wall, under a huge mirror. "Please have a seat there and I will advise the Ambassador of your arrival." His English was flawless, his German accent heavy.

He bowed again and strode away, almost as if he were marching. She smiled, her familiarity with the German people and their abrupt mannerisms was quite telling in the young man's affectation.

The room was large and airy. Floor to ceiling windows allowed quite a bit of light. The floor was marble, with an image of the German flag imbedded in the center.

Despite it being a normal workday, silence surrounded her, most likely those serving the Embassy hidden away in offices behind closed doors. Within minutes, the young man returned and once again bowed. "If you will follow me, Miss Sanford, I will take you to the Ambassador's office."

She followed him through a maze of doors and corridors. Carpet muted their footsteps, and everything remained quiet. They passed a door where she could hear a man's voice speaking in German. Nothing of interest, however.

Eventually they came to the end of a corridor and her guide rapped twice on the door in front of them.

"Eingeben!"

The young man opened the door and again bowing, waved his arm toward an immense wooden desk behind which sat the Ambassador, who rose to his feet. "Ah, Miss Sanford. How lovely to see you." He nodded at the young man. *"Du darfst gehen. Ich möchte nicht gestört warden."*

So, he did not want to be disturbed? She was sure he hadn't known she understood his command. Perhaps Dante had been right and seeing him alone might not have been a good idea. She fumbled in her reticule and wrapped her fingers around the hat pin she had slipped in there. Just in case.

Once the Ambassador was settled in his seat, he said, "May I offer you tea?" He made a face. "I don't like the drink myself, but you English seem to be in love with it. Give me a good bier." He laughed at his own joke and Lydia smiled back.

His nose was healing, but the yellow and green marks would take another week or so to fade.

"No thank you for the tea, Ambassador. I have just broken my fast."

"Ah yes, you English ladies like to, how do you say, loll about in bed?"

There was no point in arguing the point. The man had some definite ideas about her country and its residents. She was not here to act as ambassador for England. "Yes. Sometimes."

The Ambassador leaned forward in his chair and placed his arms on the desk. She was already uncomfortable with the way he kept eyeing her. "What brings you here this morning, Miss Sanford?"

She tried her sweetest, most innocuous mien. "I wish to apologize for Mr. Rose's actions at the inn last week."

The Ambassador scowled. "He is a rude man. I meant no harm. I was merely offering some attention to a beautiful young woman."

That was hardly the case, but either the Ambassador didn't remember what he'd done, or his idea of how to offer a young lady his attentions was not part of the etiquette book she'd studied with her governess.

She smiled. "I hope we can continue to be friends."

"What about Mr. Rose? Why was he so forceful?"

Lydia crossed her fingers in her lap, about to spew out falsehoods. She waved her hand in the air. "Mr. Rose is of the mind that I welcome his attentions, and therefore is of the opinion that he must be my champion." She lowered her eyelashes and looked at the Ambassador, offering a sultry smile. "Even when I do not need it."

Gads. The look he threw her almost brought up her breakfast. Perhaps she had overdone it. She only wanted to be granted access to him so she could hear his conversations, not encourage him to think there could ever be anything of an intimate nature between them.

Before she could get in any deeper, she stood. The man hopped up, also. "I believe I have taken up enough of your time."

"Not at all, Miss Sanford." He followed her as she turned and headed to the door, anxious to be away. He reached out and took her arm. "I should like you to accompany me to the theater one evening." He raised her hand to his mouth and placed a kiss there. She wanted to rub her glove against her cape.

When she didn't answer, he added. "Thursday. I shall call at your home at seven o'clock."

Since it sounded more like an order than an invitation, she nodded. "Yes. That sounds most pleasant."

The young man who had shown her to his office stood outside the door. He bowed again. Then turning on his heel, he marched off, and Lydia followed.

Oh, dear God. What had she gotten herself into? Dante would be furious. Perhaps she could beg off with a megrim. Which she probably would have by Thursday.

DANTE HOPPED from the carriage the minute he saw Lydia exit the building. She hurried up to him and gave him a strange smile.

"What did he say to you? Did he touch you?" he growled. "I'll go back in there—"

Lydia grabbed his arm and they climbed into the carriage. "Nothing bad happened. It's all fine."

The carriage began to move forward, and he straightened his jacket and glared at her. "Why do I have the feeling you're hiding something?"

She sighed and looked out the window. "The Ambassador was very gracious and accepted the apology I offered. At least I think he did." She waved her hand. "Anyway, he seemed fine."

"That was it? Nothing else happened? Why do I still think there is more to this story?"

"Because he invited me to the theater Thursday evening."

He frowned, not at all liking her demeanor. "And you said no, of course."

She glared at him. "There really was no way to say no. He just assumed I was willing and told me he would arrive at my house at seven o'clock on Thursday evening to escort me."

"I'm going, too."

"You weren't invited."

"I don't care."

"I told him there was nothing between you and me."

That brought his thoughts to an abrupt halt. He didn't like the sound of that. The only reason, of course, was because they had to work together on the assignment. Not because she seemed too comfortable with throwing that statement out there.

He would give himself time to consider that later. Right now he had a very bad feeling about the Ambassador, and it had nothing to do with the investigation. "Lydia. We must work something out. I don't like the idea of you and the Ambassador sitting in his dark box in the theater. Alone. Or his carriage, either."

"Then I will bring a chaperone."

"Excellent. I will make a wonderful chaperone."

She sighed again. "Not you. You cannot be my chaperone."

"Why not?"

"I will bring my maid."

"Does she carry a gun?"

She laughed. Actually laughed like this was a comedy and he was reciting all the funny lines. "No. My maid does not carry a gun."

"Then I shall go with you." He held up his hand. "Just hear what I have to say. Hunt has a box at the theater, so I can attend the same evening. There wouldn't be anything odd about that. I've used it before."

Her jaw tightened and she flashed an angry look in his direction. "Dante, this is becoming ridiculous. I am able to take care of myself. You act as though you suspect the man will attempt to kidnap me."

"Bloody hell." He ran his fingers through his hair. "I never thought of that." He looked up at her. "Suppose he knows about our investigation, and it is his intention to silence you?"

She stared at him with her mouth open. "You are becoming downright deranged. I know we suspect him of gaining secrets from the Home Office and passing them along to his government, but now you have him as a lecher and possibly an abductor, or murderer." She drew herself up and glared at him. "I fear you are becoming unhinged."

He huddled in the corner, arms crossed, and stared out the window. Mayhaps he was starting to sound a tad overprotective and suspicious. However, he still intended to follow the carriage from her house to the theater and then avail himself of Hunt's theater box. He had no idea where his brother's box was in relation to the Ambassador's, but if he arrived early and hung about the lobby, he could wait for them to enter, and then follow them.

'Twas probably best not to let Lydia in on his plan.

She reached over and patted him on the knee. "It will be

127

fine." She fumbled in her reticule and withdrew a hat pin. "See. I was prepared."

He laughed. And she laughed with him. The tension eased in the carriage, and they had a pleasant ride back to her house where he left her with a reminder that they were to attend the Davidson ball that evening.

Dante instructed his driver to take him to the Rose Room. He needed to get away from the investigation, the Ambassador, and most of all, Lydia.

She was driving him crazy and he was turning into a loon, acting like some sort of a besotted lover. Of course nothing untoward would happen in the dark theater box with Lydia and the lecherous Ambassador with heavy curtains between them and the rest of the theater. He had no need to worry. None at all.

Like bloody hell he didn't.

LYDIA HAD to admit she was a tad nervous as she awaited Dante's arrival for them to attend the Davidson ball that evening. Now that she had made peace between her and the Ambassador, she was concerned she'd overplayed and now the man thought she had a romantic interest in him.

Nothing could be further from the truth. Not when it was Dante who occupied her dreams, both when asleep and awake. Why had she allowed the man to get under her skin?

When they'd first met, she had a firm opinion of what he was like. His reputation had preceded him. A rake, a libertine, and a rogue. He and his two brothers, especially Hunt, had built up a reputation among the ladies of the *ton*. It had always amused her that Dante evaded the *ton*, yet he remained one of their darlings.

His bastard standing seemed to mean nothing; if anything

made him more of a reprobate. Then they were paired on the assignment and she found a funny, caring, honorable man. Certainly not what she'd been expecting.

And his kisses! She'd had her share of kisses over the years, but none moved her the way Dante's had. She'd allowed him liberties she would never have dreamed of allowing a man not her husband.

She tried to tell herself he was the same with other women and he found nothing special about her. Except she'd seen the surprise on the faces of the women he'd turned away to dance or walk with her.

It was just the investigation. He needed to make it appear as if they were courting so he had a reason to be in her company all the time so they could gather the information the Home Office needed.

"Mr. Rose has arrived." One of the footmen tapped on her bedchamber door. Lydia gathered up her things and with her shawl resting over her arm, she left the room and headed to the front parlor. Before she made it to the bottom stair, she could hear Dante and Father conversing.

This was troubling. The two of them were conversing like old friends. They both held a brandy and were quite relaxed on two chairs facing the fireplace.

Dante hopped up when she entered the room, with Father right behind him. "Good evening, Miss Sanford. You look lovely as always."

Lydia moved toward the two chairs and settled on the settee across from Dante's seat. "Thank you."

He looked as handsome and dashing as usual, with all black evening clothes, except for a white shirt and silver and black waistcoat. When he looked at her, the tiny butterflies in her stomach did a quadrille. "Would you care for a sherry before we leave?"

So now Dante was taking over Father's place as host?

"Yes, please."

Quickly and efficiently, Dante walked to the sideboard, poured her a sherry, and brought it to her. Lydia glanced at her father who viewed Dante, and the two of them, with a father's pride and happiness.

She couldn't help wondering how fast Dante could escape the room if he knew what was going on behind Father's cheerful countenance.

The three chatted for a few minutes about the ball that evening, and the musicale the following night. Lydia smartly refrained from mentioning the theater outing with the Ambassador on Thursday. Besides not wanting to put Dante in a foul mood, she also did not think Father would approve, either.

Honestly. Men seemed to think women could not make a decision for themselves, that as men they must always guide them and decide what was best. She was a grown woman and had every intention of guiding her own life.

Even if she were to marry.

Now there was a thought not as easily dismissed as it had once been. Before she would dwell on it more, however, Dante stood and took the empty glass from her hand. "Are you ready?"

"Yes." She gathered her reticule and slid on her gloves. Dante took the shawl from her and placed it over her shoulders. The warmth from his hands resting briefly on her shoulders sent shivers down her body.

"Are you cold," he asked, his lips close to her ear.

She shook her head. Goodness, Father was right in the room. She glanced sideways at him to see a bright smile.

Yes, trouble.

She kissed Father on his cheek, and they left the room. She swore he was humming under his breath when she kissed him.

"Your father is a cheerful sort," Dante said as they settled into the carriage. "I knew him from the club, of course, but never really spoke much with him."

"Yes." She pulled the shawl tighter over her shoulders. "He is quite pleasant. He has a great deal of friends. I always wondered why he never remarried. He was certainly young enough when Mother died."

"How long ago did your mother pass away?"

"I was five years old. She died giving birth to my brother, who died, as well."

"So now I have to be an un-gentleman and ask you how many years ago that was which will tell me how old you are."

Lydia grinned. She was never one to be concerned about her age. She was happily on the shelf and had been for several years. "It matters not. I am six and twenty, which means Mother passed away twenty-one years ago." She paused for a moment. "My goodness, I hadn't realized how long she is gone. I remember her quite clearly. Maybe because Father never did re-marry so there wasn't another mother to take her place in my life."

Dante shifted to rest his foot on his other knee. "I never knew my mother. Everyone knows I am the bastard son, and apparently my devoted mother had no use for me, and I was left on the earl's doorstep when I was only a few weeks old.

"My father immediately pronounced me as his son, and insisted I be raised right along Hunt and Driscoll. Their mother, naturally, wasn't too fond of the idea, but the earl insisted. While I can't say Lady Huntington was mean to me, because she was not, I never got the same warm feelings from her as my brothers did."

"Considering how many by-blows are tossed into the foundling homes, I must give Lord Huntington a great deal of credit for what he did."

"Yes." Dante nodded. "He was a remarkable man." He paused for a moment. "I loved him, and miss him every day."

Their carriage joined the queue waiting to alight at the Davidsons' townhouse. Soon a footman opened the door and Dante stepped out and turned to help Lydia.

"I will help the young lady, my boy." The Ambassador elbowed Dante out of the way and took Lydia's hand. "It's truly a pleasure to see you, Miss Sanford. As always, you are looking stunning."

Lydia inwardly groaned. This was precisely what she'd been afraid of. She looked helplessly at Dante who glowered as though he was prepared to do a repeat performance on the Ambassador's nose.

Not to be outdone, Dante stepped up to her other side and linked his arm with hers. He leaned down close to her ear. "Do not, under any circumstances, allow that man to snag a waltz. Save them for me. All of them."

Lydia groaned.

15

The three of them were all announced together and descended the stairs to the ballroom floor as one. Neither man would let go of her arm and she began to feel like she was the center of a tug of war.

They'd barely stepped foot onto the floor when Dante whipped the dance card out of her hand. He quickly wrote his name on two spots and smirked in the Ambassador's direction.

The Ambassador's turn was next. He snatched the card, crossed out Dante's name on one line and added his. Dante took the card back again and when he prepared to cross out the Ambassador's name, Lydia grabbed it back and tore it in two. "There." She took a deep breath. "Shall we stroll gentlemen?"

It was the beginning of the most frustrating and annoying night Lydia had ever endured. Neither man would leave her side, even when she said she had to visit the ladies' retiring room. They both walked her there, and even though she spent almost a half hour there, they were both propped up against the wall glaring at each other when she exited the room.

"Pardon me, Ambassador, but may I have a word with Mr. Rose?" She offered her bright smile at the man.

He glowered in Dante's direction, but nodded. Lydia dragged Dante away so they would not be heard. "This is ridiculous. The man will have no opportunity to speak with anyone else with the two of you acting like dogs hovering over a piece of meat."

"I don't trust him."

Lydia sighed and searched the heavens for an answer. "What could possibly happen in a crowded ballroom? I have no intention of leaving the room with the Ambassador and—"

"—or the garden. Don't go into the garden. Or the patio. If you need fresh air I will take you outside."

She counted to ten, then went up to thirty. "Very well. I will not leave the room. If I feel faint, I shall find you, or faint right in the middle of the floor where you can see me."

The features on his face softened and he reached up to run his finger down her cheek. "I don't want anything to happen to you. It's important to me."

She grew serious. "Why is that?"

He looked guilty, as though he hadn't meant to say what he had. "Er, because of the assignment. I need you to work with me on it." He looked away, as if uncomfortable looking at her while he murmured the words.

Lies, perhaps?

She nodded. "Fine. I will see you for our dance and fill you in on anything I've gained." She made her way back to the Ambassador who took her arm. "Is everything all right, Miss Sanford? I shall be more than happy to speak with the young man if he won't leave you alone."

Good grief.

"Everything is well, Ambassador. Let us return to the ballroom. I think it is getting close to our dance."

Things went slightly better once she'd spoken to Dante, but

he continued to dodge her heels. No matter where she stood, or who she was speaking with, one glance up and there was Dante watching her with a frown.

By the time the ball had ended, her feet hurt, she was tired of the Ambassador trying to talk her into a stroll in the garden, and quite finished with watching Dante scowl at her.

"May I escort you home, Miss Sanford," the Ambassador said.

Goodness, no.

"Thank you anyway, but Mr. Rose escorted me here, so I shall return with him."

The man leaned in close to her ear. "I don't trust him."

Counting to forty would not even help at this point. She offered what she hoped was a confident smile. "I will be fine, Ambassador. Thank you for a pleasant evening." She slipped away as quickly as she could, having no problem finding Dante since he hadn't left her view all evening.

She tugged on his arm. "Get me out of here, please. I am about to explode."

He retrieved her shawl and wrapped it around her shoulders. She practically pulled him down the steps into the waiting carriage. Once they were settled, she leaned her head back on the squab. "I am so very grateful this evening is over."

"Did he touch you!"

She looked at him through slitted eyes, not moving her head an inch. "How could he ever touch me without you knowing, since you never stopped watching us all night?" Her jaw hurt from clenching it. "What about all the dances you were supposed to have with other ladies?"

"I never signed up for any," he mumbled.

They rode in silence for a few minutes. Then Dante cleared his throat. "Did you, um, learn anything?"

Fighting a megrim, she kept her eyes closed. "No. All his conversations were in English. Except one, but that was merely an exchange of pleasantries with someone who didn't speak English well."

"Are you well?" There was genuine concern in his voice.

"As I said, I have the beginnings of a megrim."

He shifted so he sat next to her. "Here, lean against my chest and I will massage your temples."

She shifted so he could place his fingers on the side of her head. He began to gently rub, and she sighed. "Um, that feels wonderful."

* * *

THIS HAD BEEN the most frustrating and annoying evening of his life. As Dante rubbed Lydia's head, his mind went back to the obnoxious Ambassador. How he would love to punch him in the face again! Only this time he'd be sure to break the insufferable man's nose instead of just bruising it.

This was one investigation that he would be more than happy to uncover information to ruin the man. Send him back to where he came from in disgrace. He'd watched him and Lydia all evening and even though nothing improper—that he could see—took place, he hated the proprietary air the Ambassador had toward Lydia.

Lydia shifted on his body and moaned. His blood immediately flowed south to cause an instant erection. Hopefully, she wouldn't notice. He'd finally admitted to himself at the blasted ball that his interest in keeping Lydia safe had very little to do with the assignment and a great deal to do with his growing feelings for her.

Each time she smiled at the Ambassador, or even any other man, he had the urge to march over there, grab her by the arm and announce to all and sundry that she was his. He could only imagine how well that would have gone over with his independent Lydia. She most likely would have broken *his* nose.

She moaned once again, and he reached down to kiss her forehead. "Does that feel better?"

"Oh. Yes. Definitely yes. You do such a good job of rubbing."

He nearly swallowed his tongue. "I would love to show you what a good job of rubbing I could do. It would bring you great pleasure."

"Oh?" She shifted a bit to look up at him. "What do you mean?"

"Actually, sweeting, it would involve the removal of clothing and take place somewhere that would not roll up to the front of your house."

She shifted so she was lying across his lap. "I think I know what you mean."

"Of course you do. You are an intelligent woman."

They stared at each other, the gas lights from the street illuminating their faces, then throwing them into darkness as they moved down the street. Dante pulled the curtain on both sides of the carriage closed.

"What are you doing?"

Instead of answering her, he lowered his head and took her mouth with all the possession he'd been fighting all evening. He nudged her lips with his tongue, and she opened to him.

Sweet. Moist. Warm. She tasted like champagne and something sweet. She joined him in the duel and they savored each other's mouths. He shifted her once again and moved his hand up to cup her breast. His thumb slid back and forth over her nipple, which was begging for release.

Always the gentleman, he complied by loosening the back of her gown and pulled at the shoulders until her breasts were revealed, plump and firm above her stays. He leaned down and kissed the quivering flesh, and then with a flick of his tongue slid over the already aroused nipple.

Lydia grabbed his arm. "Oh, my. That feels good."

Years of practice had him untying the front of her stays in

an instant and opening the sides to view her beauty. He drew back and sucked in a breath, wishing he hadn't closed the curtains. "You are beautiful, Lydia." He took one of her breasts in his mouth and suckled.

Not one to be shy, she reached between them and rubbed her palm over his cock. "Did I do this to you?"

"Oh, yes." If she kept that up he would end up plunging into her and taking her innocence right there in the carriage. While moving.

His eyes jerked open at that thought. The carriage was no longer moving, and he could feel the driver jump from the seat.

"Lydia, love. Quickly, up."

"What?" Her eyes were glazed as she didn't seem able to focus.

He reached for the door handle just as the driver arrived. "Just give us a moment, John. Miss Sanford is feeling a bit lightheaded."

"Yes, Mr. Rose."

"You may return to your seat. We will be out in a minute."

That was definitely a snort he heard coming from John. Hopefully Lydia hadn't heard it. He glanced over at her, and she appeared confused. He quickly tied her stays as best he could, spun her around on the seat and fastened the back of her gown.

"There, sweeting. You look somewhat presentable."

She reached up to her head. "My hair? Is it a mess?"

He tucked the loosened curls behind her ears and attempted to pat down the rest of it, to at least make it look a little bit better. "It's fine. Come, let's go."

He exited the carriage and turned to take her hand. "How is your headache?"

"Gone, I think."

They made their way up the steps and the front door immediately opened. Hopefully Lord Sterling would not be about to see his daughter arrive home in her disheveled state.

The butler bowed. "Good evening, Miss Sanford, Mr. Rose."

Lydia turned to him, still appearing a bit dazed. "Would you care for a drink, Mr. Rose?"

Wanting her to retire to her bedchamber before anyone could take a good look at her, he declined. "I will see you tomorrow for the musicale?"

"No need. The Ambassador mentioned this evening that he would not be attending the musicale tomorrow, but he would be here Thursday to escort me to the theater."

Remembering that dreaded theater outing, he scowled. "And I will be there as well."

"Inconspicuous, I hope," she said.

"You will never know I'm there."

They had stepped inside to get out of the evening air, but thankfully her father had not made an appearance, and the well-trained butler had disappeared.

"You best retire before anyone sees you."

Her eyes grew wide and she patted her hair again. "Do I look that bad?"

"You look beautiful." He pulled her into his arms and kissed her, and had to force himself to stop.

"Will you work at your club tomorrow since there's no reason to attend the musicale?"

"Yes. Driscoll could always use a break."

Lydia gave a curt nod. "Excellent. What time will you pick me up?"

Dante groaned. Another night fighting with himself to keep his hands off Miss Sanford's delectable body. "I don't suppose you will accept a night off to do things that young ladies do when they have a night off?"

She grinned and shook her head. "No, I'm afraid not. And you know your brother could use the help with the books."

That, unfortunately was true since the investigation was

taking longer than he'd anticipated. "Very well. I will arrive around eight tomorrow evening."

* * *

LYDIA AND DANTE hustled from the carriage to the back door of the Rose Room. It amused her how familiar the club was beginning to feel to her. They immediately went their separate ways. Dante to the gaming floor and Lydia to the staff dining room.

While Dante had told her that she was free to use the dining room on the office floor as he and Driscoll did, when she was not with one of them, she felt more comfortable among those who worked at the club. Which was a surprise to her since she'd never associated with working class people before.

Even though Driscoll and Dante were by definition working men, they still had the aura of the Beau Monde about them due to their connection to the Earl of Huntington.

She'd passed up dinner at home since Father was away for the evening and rather than eat alone, she decided to wait until she got to the club.

"Hello, Miss Sanford. It's always nice to see you." Mr. Fallen, one of the security guards greeted her as she entered the room. The sideboard was filled with dishes, the scent wafting through the air, reminding her how hungry she was since she'd skipped tea earlier.

"It is very nice to see you as well, Mr. Fallen. How is the little one doing?" The last time she'd worked he'd told her his young son was suffering from some sort of an ague.

"Much better, thank you. Oftentimes the little ones recover quite quickly."

"I'm happy to hear that." She walked to the sideboard and eyed the array of food. Whitefish in some sort of a delicious smelling sauce, along with roasted beef, root vegetables in another sauce, two different potato offerings and an entire section devoted to pies, tarts, and biscuits were laid out in an enticing manner.

They ate well at the Rose Room.

Lydia was just finishing her coffee that had washed down a delicious slice of Charlotte Russe, when Dante entered the room.

"What brings you down here with us lowly ones?" Mr. Fallen asked.

"I know what brings him here," Sally, one of the maids said. "Mr. Rose has a fancy for Miss Sanford."

Gertrude, another maid, laughed out loud as she stood. "Our Mr. Rose? Never. He wouldn't give up all his ladies for only one. No. I don't believe it."

Lydia felt her face growing red. Dante smiled at the women —his natural response to anything female Lydia had noticed, and then sat next to her. He waved in their direction. "Off with you. There is work to be done."

Once they left the room he said, "It seems the reason the Ambassador gave up his night at the musicale was to have an evening of gaming here at the Rose Room."

"Truly?"

"Yes. He sent word that he would like his usual chair at the *vingt-et-un* table reserved for him." Dante ran his fingers through his hair. "It looks as though your request to again deal at the table has been granted."

Lydia perked up. As much as she liked helping the men out by doing Driscoll's work when she was able, she truly loved the excitement of being on the gaming floor and especially working at the table.

"That's wonderful. Well, I'm sure you don't think so, but I've been waiting for another chance to give it a try."

"The problem is your outfit." He waved his hand up and down her sensible blue light wool dress, hardly anything like the one she wore the last time she dealt. But then there hadn't been any reason to expect to need anything different this time to merely work on the books.

"Yes. I see what you mean."

"I told you we kept gowns along with the masks for the employees to use when we hold our annual ball. I'll have one of the maids accompany you downstairs to where they are stored and help you find one and get you into it. I still have the mask you used the last time."

"Now?"

Dante checked his timepiece. "Yes. The club will open in about a half hour. Can you be ready by then?"

"Yes." There was no doubt in her mind that she could slip into something different and don a mask again. What she needed time for was refreshing her memory on dealing. She'd ask a couple of the other employees to work with her to gain her confidence back.

He stood and pulled out her chair. "Come. I will find someone to help you."

"I would also like a few others to play the game so I can refresh my memory."

"That is a good idea." He placed his palm at her lower back and steered her out of the dining room into the kitchen. There he found a maid to take her downstairs to change into a gown and ask her to round up a few employees that would be free until the club opened to work with Lydia on the dealing.

She was excited to be back dealing again. Before she'd gotten a chance to say anything else to Dante, he was gone, leaving her with the maid and a wardrobe full of gowns.

She rifled through them and came up with a red satin gown, black lace along the neckline, the end of the sleeves and the hem. She held in up against her body and looked into the full-length mirror. "Perfect."

Sally had been the one designated to help her into the

gown. When she looked at Lydia with the garment against her, she shook her head and smiled. "Mr. Rose might want to tell himself he doesn't have a fancy for you, but I guarantee one look at you in that gown, and he will declare himself for all of London to hear."

16

*D*espite the little bit of practice Lydia had with two of the maids and one security guard at the upstairs dining room table, she still fought the butterflies in her stomach as she walked with Dante to the *vingt-et-un* table.

"You seem nervous," Dante said.

"Yes. I am a bit. But I'm sure once I get started, I will be fine." She looked up at him as he studied her. "That is why I should do this more often."

He gave a soft laugh. "Nice attempt, Miss Sanford, but once this assignment is over, you won't be dealing cards at the Rose Room anymore."

She was surprised at how saddened she felt at his statement. Did that mean she would never see him anymore, either? As she moved to take her position behind the table, she had to fight the tears attempting to force their way out. It would never do to have him see her so weak. If the end of the assignment meant the end of their relationship, then so be it.

What did she expect, that Dante was so smitten that he would begin attending *ton* events—that he loathed—just to spend time with her? Most likely he was anxious to get back to all the ladies he'd been rebuffing.

Oh, Lord, now she truly was going to cry.

"Is something wrong, sweeting?"

Don't call me that. I'm not one of your lightskirts.

She smiled, blinking rapidly. "Not at all. I had something in my eye, but I think it's gone now."

Either Dante knew her better than she thought, or her ability to conceal her feelings had diminished. He looked at her with concern, which only made her feel worse. She needed to get away from him. Now. Before she made a complete cake of herself. "You can go about your duties. I will be fine." Ignoring him, she took out two decks of cards and placed them on the table where the punters would see them before she opened the packs.

He hesitated, then said, "Very well. However, if anything happens that I should know about, signal me in some way. I will be watching your table on and off all night."

She nodded and continued to shuffle. She breathed a sigh of relief when one of the security guards called him and he left to deal with that issue. Lydia checked her timepiece. The club was set to open any minute. She needed to get herself under control. She had a job to do. Well, actually two jobs. She needed to be a skilled *vingt-et-un* dealer and work on the assignment for the Home Office.

You are a professional, Lydia. Keep yourself focused.

SHE HAD BEEN DEALING for about forty-five minutes when the Ambassador appeared at her table. He'd not recognized her the last time she dealt, but she had spent more time with him since then.

Apparently, not expecting to see a woman of the Beau Monde standing behind a table at a gaming club, whipping cards to players, he briefly nodded to her and settled into the seat that had remained empty since they'd opened with a 'reserved' sign on it.

When the game they had been in the middle of finished, she nodded at him and dealt to the five players sitting in a semi-circle in front of her. It hadn't taken her long to become fast and efficient. By the third game it was as if she'd done this all her life.

The Ambassador had a footman bring him a drink, which he quickly downed and then signaled for another one. His playing remained astute, however, and he won a couple of hands.

She'd just raked in the cards from a game when a woman walked up to the table and placed her hands on the Ambassador's shoulders. She was a pretty woman, but one who had obviously been relying on face makeup to hide her age. Since Dante had told her ladies were not welcomed at the club, but men could bring their mistresses and courtesans, this woman's low-cut gown and presence at the club signaled her status.

The Ambassador patted one of her hands. She leaned down to speak with him, but he waved her off as he watched the cards being dealt. Once he had his cards in front of him, he moved his chair back and she climbed onto his lap. Not bothering to keep his voice down, he said, *"U tebya yest' moya infor-matsiya?"*

She smiled and twirled a bit of his hair with her finger. *"U tebya yest' moi den'gi?"*

He scowled and pulled his head back. *"Zavtra vecherom v Adel'fi teatre. V kholle cherez desyat' minut postle predstavleniye nachala."* He shoved her off his lap and picked up the card Lydia had just dealt him. The woman sauntered away with a smirk on her face.

Lydia quickly translated the Russian in her head.

"Do you have my information?"

"Do you have my money?"

"Tomorrow night at the Adelphi theater. In the lobby ten minutes after the performance starts."

Lydia almost screamed with excitement. This was what they'd been waiting for! She looked around the room while trying to keep her mind on the game. Dante leaned one shoulder against the wall while he spoke with Keniel.

She cleared her throat which was silly since the noise of the club would certainly deaden any sound she made. She looked at the wall closest to her. One of the security guards stood watching her, his arms crossed. She nodded in his direction.

He strolled over to her table. "Yes, miss?"

"Please fetch Mr. Rose. I need to speak with him immediately."

"He's busy now. Maybe I can help."

She glared at him. "He is over there," she gestured with her head, "talking to Keniel. I'm sure if you tell him I need to speak with him, he will heed you."

The guard looked her up and down with a lecherous glance that had her skin crawling.

"Just go."

"Are we going to play, or chat all night?" one of the players at the table said.

"My apology," she answered with a strong French accent, which she'd been using all evening since she'd spoken only French to the Ambassador at his last visit. She began dealing again and tried her best to tamp down her excitement.

Within minutes Dante was standing next to her. "What is it?"

She kept her eyes on the cards. "I need a break."

He studied her for a minute. "Very well. I will have Malcolm take over."

She nodded. "If you will join me upstairs in the office?"

He seemed to pick up on her agitation. "Yes. I could use a break myself."

It took about ten minutes to make all the switches to allow Lydia to raise her hands to the players and step back to leave the table. A couple of the gamers complained that she was bringing them good luck and didn't want her to leave. Since he'd been losing, the Ambassador was not one of them.

* * *

DANTE WAS SITTING in the office, his feet up on the desk when Lydia came flying in. "It has happened!" She stopped to take a deep breath. "The contact has been made."

He nodded to the chair in front of his desk. "Take a minute to catch your breath."

"I will," she panted.

Dante got up and poured her a glass of water from the pitcher on the table near the back of the room. "Here, drink this."

She nodded and took the glass from his hand. After taking a few sips, she placed it on the desk. "We were looking for a man to make the contact with the Ambassador, but it was a woman."

A woman? Dante raised his brows. "Start at the beginning."

She quickly went through what had happened at the table. He sat stunned as she went through the scenario. He had to admit it had taken him by surprise. "A courtesan? All this time?" He stood and began to pace. "How the devil does someone like her get Crown secrets?"

Lydia shrugged. "Having very little contact with someone of her ilk, I could not say, but don't men tend to say things when they are . . ."

Despite the situation, Dante had to grin. "When they are what?"

She waved her hand. "You know."

He placed his hand on his chest and attempted to look surprised. "Do you think I would know what you're referring to, Miss Sanford? Me? Innocent me?"

She scowled at him. "Do I need to slap you on the head?"

He pulled up a chair and swung it around, sitting so his arms rested on the back of the chair. "That would have to be the only way she could get secrets like that. Now we have to decide what to do."

"Go to the theater, of course."

"Yes. But we need to set a few things up. First of all, Sir Phillip must be advised. He will want someone in authority there when the switch takes place."

"Of course."

"Now that we know the transfer of information will be done at the theater, I am even more reluctant to have you attend with the Ambassador. This could be a serious and possibly dangerous situation."

"No. I have to go. We need to behave as if nothing is wrong. I'm even a little concerned that I left the table shortly after the conversation between him and the woman took place."

Dante leaned his chin on his fisted hands. "He has no way of knowing the dealer was you. And you said they conversed in Russian. How many card dealers would be familiar with Russian?"

"I guess I'm just a bit jumpy at finally having something to work on." She looked around the room. "I could use a cup of tea right now."

What he could use was a snifter of brandy, and Lydia spread out on the bed in the bedchamber down the hall from them. Sans clothing. But that idea was wrong. Very, very wrong.

He stood. "Come, let us see if there is hot tea in the dining room. If not, there is tea downstairs at the buffet table, although the men who avail themselves of the food and drink rarely opt for tea."

"How can you be so calm? I am beside myself with excitement."

They entered and left the dining room quickly since there was no tea to be had there. They made their way downstairs to the gaming floor. He led her over to the buffet table and Lydia quickly made her cup of tea. She shook her head no when he pointed to the table of biscuits and sweet treats.

Dante snagged a brandy from the bar and they made their way back upstairs. He stared at Lydia as he sipped his brandy. She removed her mask and was flushed with excitement, something he would like to see in the bedchamber a few doors down.

He really had to take his mind far from those thoughts. As they sat in amicable silence, he pondered exactly where he and Lydia were in their relationship? Friendship? Partnership? Which was it? And which one did he want it to be?

So many questions and so few answers. He'd never wanted a permanent relationship. With no need for heirs, he expected to spend his life unmarried. He'd never felt the need to share his life with someone.

And then Lydia had arrived in his life. The Lydia he met with his arrogance and dislike had changed into the Lydia he not only enjoyed spending time with but of whom he'd found himself feeling quite possessive.

Aside from that, she was a beautiful woman with a body that was made for loving. Given what he'd learned so far, he had no doubts that she would be an enthusiastic bed partner. But she was a lady. Ladies did not have affairs unless they were very discreet widows.

As much as he'd wanted to fit her into the typical *ton* category—flighty, gossipy, impressed with money and titles—she was none of those things. The devil take it, the woman just translated in her head a conversation in Russian!

No she was not your typical *ton* female.

Then, where did that leave them? He truly did not want to shake her hand and say goodbye when the assignment ended. From what he'd seen of her reaction to him and his kisses so far, he doubted she wanted it to end, either.

But what, exactly, was *it*?

* * *

LYDIA PACED IN HER BEDCHAMBER, her skirts swirling as she turned to walk one way, then another. The Ambassador would arrive within the next few minutes to escort her to the theater.

According to the plan they'd devised with Sir Phillip, he would have sworn officers unknown to anyone from the Home Office in the theater lobby, posing as footmen.

Dante would be in the lobby as well, and she would be with the Ambassador in his theater box. She was assuming once the performance began he would leave to meet his contact in the lobby. If all went well, it would be accomplished in a matter of minutes, with both the Ambassador and the woman he was meeting, in handcuffs and led from the building.

Then it would be over.

And it was that thought making her pace. Not the excitement of bringing down the Ambassador—much to her chagrin since she prided herself on her work—but the thought of after weeks of being together, she and Dante would most likely go their separate ways.

Before she could twist herself completely into knots, there was a slight knock on her door. "The Ambassador has arrived, Miss Sanford."

She thanked the maid and grabbing her reticule and shawl, left her room and headed downstairs. Father stood in the entrance hall, speaking with the Ambassador. She'd told her father a bit about their investigation. Not enough to compromise it, but just so he would know the Ambassador escorting her to the theater was not to be considered noteworthy.

Of course, Father had surprised her by clearly stating that in his opinion, Mr. Dante Rose was a much better catch than the Ambassador.

Not that Dante was swimming around, waiting for someone to 'catch' him, she'd retorted. Father just gave her one of those enigmatic smiles and whistling an off-key tune, walked away.

The Ambassador looked up as she descended. Due to Dante's concerns, and truth be told, her own as well, she wore a reasonably modest gown. The neckline was certainly high enough to discourage too much leering. She had also tucked her ever-ready hat pin into her reticule.

He bowed and took her hand. She was grateful that she'd already put on her gloves as he slobbered over her hand in a kiss. "You are beautiful, Miss Sanford. I am honored that you have allowed me to escort you to the theater this evening."

"Thank you, Mr. Ambassador."

He took her arm and tucked it into his, pressing her body next to his. She moved slightly so they weren't touching. It certainly did not feel as it did when Dante had done the same thing.

Dante's form was muscular, where the Ambassador's was soft. Dante smelled of bergamot while the Ambassador smelled of onions.

Now that they were on their way and she knew what the evening would bring, the butterflies had returned to her stomach.

Dante was nowhere to be seen when they entered the lobby. Lydia examined the footmen, wondering which ones were officers of the law. Everything seemed perfectly normal, but she still felt shaken inside. If only Dante were here, just one glance at him would calm her.

"Would you care for a glass of wine, Miss Sanford? Or perhaps some lemonade?"

She was quite thirsty, but with how tight her muscles felt, she doubted she would be able to swallow anything. "No. But thank you."

He strolled them over to the table where the drinks were being served. "No whisky?" He picked up a glass of sherry and glowered at the footman, as if the poor man was responsible for the lack of drink the Ambassador preferred.

They made light chatter, with other people stopping by and speaking with them. There was more than one quelling glance at seeing the two of them together.

Just as the footman announced the attendees should find their seats, she spotted Dante leaning against the far wall, his eyes boring into hers. He offered her a slight salute and a smile. He then turned and sauntered with the rest of the crowd to their seats.

He climbed the stairs, going to Hunt's box, she assumed. She and the Ambassador moved smoothly with the crowd to the upper floor, where he opened the heavy black curtain to his box, and she stepped in.

Good grief, she felt as though she were about to swoon. And she never swooned. She really had to get herself under control and act as though this was just like any other night at the theater.

They took seats near the front of the box, the Ambassador grasping her hand and setting it on his thigh. Had she not known he would be disappearing within ten minutes, she might have run screaming from her seat. The last thing she wanted was for her hand to be anywhere near his man parts.

Her heart pounded so rapidly she swore he must have heard it. In fact, they must have heard it in the box next to them.

"Are you looking forward to the play, my dear?"

My dear? Oh good heavens, how could ten minutes take so

long? She nodded and furtively patted the sweat from her upper lip with her lace-edged handkerchief and took a deep breath.

Finally, the orchestra began to play and after a few minutes the curtains opened, and the play began. As planned, about ten minutes into the performance, the Ambassador leaned over to her, his warm malodorous breath wafting over her. "I'm afraid I must make a quick visit to someone." He raised her hand again and kissed it, staring into her eyes. "I shall be right back, my dear. Enjoy the show while I am gone. I have a wonderful surprise for you when it is over."

And I have a not-so-wonderful surprise for you in a few minutes.

17

*D*ante reached the lobby no more than five minutes after the curtain had raised on the play. There were a few stragglers who had hurried across the room to either boxes on the next level or seats in the main area of the theater.

His instructions from Sir Phillip had been to be present to witness the exchange of information, but not to involve himself in it. He'd been assured there were several men posing as footmen who would arrest the Ambassador and his female partner.

Lydia was to wait in the Ambassador's box until Dante fetched her. For that he was grateful. Just in case something went awry and violence broke out he didn't want her anywhere near the lobby. She hadn't been too happy to hear that news, and it was only after he'd showed her Sir Phillip's missive with the instructions that she'd yielded to the order and agreed to remain hidden.

He took up a position against the wall across from the entrance. The woman who Lydia had described entered the lobby and smiled brightly at the man at the door. Instead of moving to a box or seat, she strolled the lobby, attempting to look as if she waited for someone.

That had to be the woman to pass information to the Ambassador. Dante looked from footman to footman, but none of them appeared to be anything but theater employees. But then, he was certain he didn't look like a government spy ready to take down the Ambassador of Germany.

His heart sped up when the Ambassador hurried down the stairs from the upper level. He looked around and with Dante concealed behind a large potted plant, the man seemed assured that all was well.

They spoke in what Dante assumed was Russian, of which he didn't understand a word. Lydia would be of use now, but since she was ordered to stay far from the exchange, nothing could be done for it. However, he wasn't interested in what they were saying, only in witnessing the exchange.

The couple seemed to argue, but eventually, the Ambassador withdrew an envelope from his jacket pocket. The woman opened it and after examining it thoroughly, she stuffed it into her reticule.

Looking annoyed, the Ambassador held his hand out. The woman handed him what appeared to be several papers. He glanced through them, a smile on his face. He nodded in her direction and turned toward the stairs.

The woman moved to the door and was immediately stopped by the footman there. Two other men seemed to appear from nowhere and blocked the Ambassador's attempt to climb the stairs.

It took about ten minutes for the Home Office men to convince the Ambassador to go with them. The woman and the other man at the door had disappeared almost as soon as he'd blocked her from leaving.

There was a great deal of shouting on the part of the Ambassador, as well as threats and other consequences for the men to be accosting him in the lobby of the theater. Eventually, they all moved from the lobby and out the door.

It was finished.

In the morning, he would write up his report for Sir Phillip and have it delivered to him. No doubt there would be a summons for him and most likely Lydia as well to appear at the man's office post haste.

His usual sense of relief when an assignment ended successfully was simply not there. No feeling of satisfaction, of being happy and anxious to get back to his normal life. His 'no Lydia' life.

He shook his head and began the climb to the upper floor. The footman had provided him with the information on which box was the Ambassador's where Lydia waited. The time had come to tell her the assignment was over. They could now part ways. Resume their lives as they were before they'd received the summons from Sir Phillip to entangle themselves into the German Ambassador's life.

He dragged his feet, giving himself time to consider what it all meant. How had his feelings for Lydia changed since they'd sat in front of Sir Phillip's desk all those weeks ago and learned they were to work together? He'd thought her a prissy female who looked down on anything male. A spinster who loathed him and all he stood for.

Over time, he'd found her to be smart, witty, kind and oh, so desirable. And quite receptive to his attentions. With the end near, the time had come to examine the feelings he'd been pushing back for weeks while telling himself there was no reason to examine them since they had work to do.

The work had ended. He reached for the curtain to the Ambassador's theater box and drew it back.

* * *

LYDIA TRIED her best to concentrate on the play since there was nothing for her to do until Dante arrived to tell her the exchange had been completed and the Ambassador and the woman were under arrest. Or whatever they called it when an Ambassador from another country was taken into custody.

She couldn't help but grin at the thought of the pompous man's reaction when he was detained and hustled from the theater.

Fidgeting in her seat, unable to think of anything except what was going on downstairs, she stood and moved to the back of the box where she was quite certain she could not be seen by other theater attendees. It was dark enough back there that she could hide.

And fret.

Her fretting began with the orders from Sir Phillip that she was not to involve herself in the exchange of information. Truthfully, when Dante first told her she would have to remain up in the theater box when the exchange took place, she balked. A typical male response. He was the big, bad man who could watch it all happen, but she was the weak, swooning female who must be protected from it.

Then when he showed her the instructions and orders from Sir Phillip where it had been clearly stated that she was to remain on the upper floor, she'd conceded. Not that she liked it any more, but at least it wasn't Dante playing the protector again.

As she wandered the small space she thought about what was going on downstairs. Did it all go peacefully? Did the Ambassador carry a pistol? Had the woman even shown up? Lord, she certainly hoped so since she'd had no intention of spending the rest of the evening with the Ambassador. Especially when he'd mentioned the wonderful surprise he had for her. She shivered at the thought of what it might be.

She moved toward the curtain and peeked out. No noise, no

shouting, no sound of a pistol going off. She checked her time-piece, but since it was dark, she couldn't see it. Hopefully it would all go smoothly. And the assignment would end.

No more Dante.

No more *ton* events with Dante.

No more working at the Rose Room with Dante.

No more kisses from Dante.

No more anything else with Dante.

A sense of depression washed over her as if she stood in bright sunlight and a dark cloud passed over the sun. Perhaps it was time to admit her feelings for the man went beyond a partnership. She continued to pace. If that were true, then where did that leave her? With a broken heart?

Dante was well known for his adamant position on marriage. It was not for him. Although he hadn't spent time with the Beau Monde, his reputation certainly did. One thing that everyone had agreed on was Mr. Dante Rose would never commit to one woman. He'd apparently voiced that opinion numerous times.

He desired her. That was obvious. And perhaps he desired numerous women over the years, but she was willing to bet that he'd never spoken with a woman the way they had, or discussed the things they'd discussed with a woman. Would that make a difference to a man like Dante?

She took in a deep breath when the curtain parted and the man taking up all her thoughts entered the theater box.

They stood staring at each other for what seemed a lifetime. Finally, she gained her voice. "Is it over?"

He nodded and walked nearer, the curtain swinging closed behind him. "Yes. He was arrested and removed from the building. The woman was also taken away."

"Ah." Instead of the joy she should feel, she felt empty. "So that's it, then."

"Yes."

That one word crushed her, not that she'd expected him to say anything different. She took a deep breath. "Then I guess we should leave." She turned and picked up her shawl and reticule, blinking furiously at her stupidity.

"Lydia."

"What." She didn't turn around. She couldn't let him see her heart was breaking.

"Look at me." His voice was low and very, very close. She could feel his warm breath, smell his intoxicating scent.

She shook her head, unable to say a word without her voice giving away her distress.

"Please." He placed his hands on her shoulders and turned her. She stared at his chest before he used his finger to lift her chin. "Do you want it to be over?"

She looked up at him and licked her dry lips. "The assignment?"

Slowly he shook his head, then pulled her toward him, his strong arms wrapped around her waist. "What do you think I mean?"

Was she going to have to be the first one to state feelings? So unfair. He'd tossed off enough women to fill a ballroom. Thinking he wouldn't do the same thing to her had been the most ludicrous thought she'd ever had.

"I don't know what to say." She truly didn't. Should she tell him how crushing the idea of not seeing him again was? Perhaps she should be the strong, independent woman she'd thought herself to be before encountering Dante and shrug and say, *Yes, it is over. Let's shake hands and depart. I have a life to live and so do you.*

He slid his palms from her waist up her back, moving her so she leaned against him. "Maybe instead of talking, we should be doing this." He lowered his head and took her mouth in a searing kiss. His warm hand cupped her face and held it gently, moving her head back and forth, taking the kiss deeper.

She succumbed to the forceful domination of his lips, his hands, his caresses. Yes. This was what she wanted. And, no she did not want it to end. But, alas, she was not alone in the decision.

Her thoughts spun as he continued his assault, withdrawing from her mouth and kissing her eyes, nose, chin, then his mouth moved to the sensitive skin under her ear. "I want you, Lydia. I've wanted you for weeks."

His words barely penetrated the fog he'd caused. Yes, she knew he desired her as she desired him. That had been apparent for a while, but what next? An affair? As much as it would devastate her to walk away, she could not commit to a liaison. The only thing that would lead to was true heartbreak when he decided he'd had enough of her and moved on to another woman.

'Twas better to get the heartbreak over now before things went too far. She pulled back and looked into his eyes. "What do you want from me, Dante?"

He opened his mouth to speak just as the curtain behind them parted and three women appeared.

"Ambassador, I just heard the most ridiculous thing..." Lady Barlow stared at them wide-eyed. "Well, I never. What is going on in here? Where is the Ambassador, and what are you two doing in here, alone, in that disgraceful embrace?"

Shocked gasps from Mrs. Winters and Lady Bolling followed Lady Barlow's words. Three of the *ton's* most vicious and gleeful gossips.

Lydia leaned her forehead on Dante's chest and groaned.

* * *

DANTE CLOSED his eyes and he cursed. *Bloody, bloody hell.*

As most young men of the Upper Crust, he'd avoided being caught with an innocent woman all his life. True, he didn't spend much time with those kinds of women, anyway, so the chance of him getting 'caught' in the parson's noose had been slight.

Only now he realized the lights had come up in the theater. It was time for intermission and based on the ladies' visit, he guessed word had somehow spread about the Ambassador.

He turned and faced the execution squad, keeping a shivering Lydia tucked into his side. "Can I help you ladies?"

Lady Barlow raised herself up and sniffed. "You certainly can, young man. We came here to speak with the Ambassador since we heard certain untruths about him. But, instead, we find you and Miss Sanford together, alone, in a dark theater box. Kissing!"

"Yes, my lady. You certainly did. However, you must allow us a bit of celebration since Miss Sanford has just done me the honor of accepting my hand in marriage."

He squeezed Lydia when she opened her mouth to speak. "Quiet, my dear," he murmured.

"Indeed?" She looked back at the other two ladies, who smirked. "I am not sure about that, Mr. Rose, but aside from your disgraceful behavior, which I am sure will reach your brother, the Earl of Huntington's ears—"

"—I am sure."

"—we are here to see the Ambassador."

He ran his palm up and down Lydia's arm, hopefully to ease her a bit. Her shaking was becoming noticeable to the ladies. "I'm afraid you will be disappointed, my lady. The Ambassador had to leave."

He had to get them out of here before the crowd grew. He could see two men and another woman standing at the entrance to the Ambassador's theater box. "If you will excuse me, I'm afraid my betrothed has developed a megrim and I must see her home."

He moved them both forward, almost having to elbow Lady Barlow for her to allow them to pass.

"I assume you will be visiting with Lord Sterling in the morning, Mr. Rose?" Lady Barlow sniffed again.

"Not that it is any concern of yours, but I assure you, my lady, I am well aware of how the procedure works, having two brothers."

"Well, I never."

"I'm quite sure you never have. Good evening ladies, gentlemen."

He hustled Lydia out of the box, down the stairs, through the lobby and outside. They passed clusters of people speaking in hushed tones, mostly about the Ambassador he was sure, but with a few glances cast their way, word of their situation must have leaked out. It amazed him how gossip seemed to spread so quickly without it even seeming physically possible.

Lydia continued to shake as they awaited the carriage. He removed his jacket and placed it over her shoulders, then pulled her against him. "Hold your head up, sweeting. Do not allow these harpies get the best of you. You are a viscount's daughter."

She merely shook her head, tears that she'd been holding sliding down her cheeks. He wanted more than anything to put her into the carriage and go back and throttle those horrible, judgmental women.

Once they were settled and he tapped on the ceiling to alert his driver to move forward, he pulled Lydia over to his side. "It will be all right."

She moved away from him, accepting the handkerchief he handed her. "No, it won't. What are we going to do now?"

Dante leaned back and rested his foot on his other knee. "I believe you heard the conversation between me and the ladies. I will visit with your father first thing tomorrow morning."

Lydia wiped her nose and smirked. "Oh, surely you don't think I believe that?"

"Why not?" Truth be known, instead of feeling 'caught' or angry at the judgemental women finding them in the Ambassador's box, to his amazement, he'd actually experienced a sense of relief. He no longer had to wrestle with his feelings and decisions. The matter had been solved for him. For them.

They must marry. Despite Lydia being of an age considered on the shelf or a spinster, she was still the daughter of a viscount, an innocent, and someone whose reputation would never survive if they did not wed.

"Dante." Her voice came out muffled, mostly from crying. "I know you have no intention of ever marrying. You've said it numerous times. The last thing I want to do is marry someone who was forced into it." She shook her head. "No. I don't care about my reputation. 'Tis a blessing, actually. Now I can stop going to those endless balls and musicales."

He leaned back on the seat, attempting to look indifferent. Certainly not how he felt. "I see. And if you are shunned by society and do not attend all the balls and musicales, what do you plan to do with the rest of your life?"

She raised her chin and he immediately had to quell the urge to laugh. She looked very much like the old Lydia he'd first met. "I shall work."

"Indeed. And what will your employment endeavors encompass?" No matter how hard he tried he couldn't hide his smile.

"Well. There are many things I can do."

This was becoming more amusing. "Such as." He waved his hand at her.

"I can teach." She nodded. "Yes. I will seek a job as a governess or tutor."

He shook his head. "I'm afraid not, sweeting. With disgrace in your background who do you think will employ you?"

"Oh." She slumped and then glanced at him sideways. "I can work at the Rose Room."

"No." He sat up and scowled at her. "Absolutely not."

"Why not?" She sniffed. "I've worked there before. I can deal cards. I can continue doing the books."

"No. And that is final."

She frowned. "Again, why not?"

"Because you worked there when you were not my wife. My wife will not work at the club. Or anywhere else for that matter." He pulled her into his arms. "The matter is settled. I will visit with Viscount Sterling in the morning, obtain a special license and we shall be married."

Strange how those words sat so well with him.

My wife.

18

"*D*ante, open the bloody door!"

Dante turned over in his bed and stared at the door to his bachelor flat. "What the hell is going on?"

"If I have to break this damn door down, I will."

He threw off the blanket and stomped to the door, ready to pummel whoever it was on the other side making that racket. For an instant it sounded like his brother, Hunt.

Dante flung the door opened. "What?" He was immediately met with his brother's fist to his face. He reeled back but caught himself from falling to the floor by grabbing the table next to him.

He swung back at his brother, but missed him, most likely because he was still half asleep and naked as the day he was born. He moved his jaw and glared at Hunt. "What the hell is this all about?"

Hunt moved into the room and looked him up and down with disgust. "Put some clothes on."

Dante immediately reached for the top hat sitting on the table and plopped it on his head. "There, I have clothes on."

Hunt gritted his teeth. "Don't make me hit you again."

"Don't try it, big brother. You caught me unaware the first time, but if you try that again, you'll find yourself flat on your back." He walked away and grabbed his trousers from the chair alongside his bed and pulled them on.

"Now to what do I owe the honor of this visit?" Not trusting his brother not to try to hit him again, he stood with his fists at his side.

"Relax, Dante. I came to talk to you."

"Really? How interesting. All I've witnessed so far is shouting, threatening and a cuff to my jaw." He waved to his rumpled bed. "Won't you have a seat?"

"No. I'm not going to be here long."

"Thank God."

Hunt pointed his finger at him. "Don't bait me, brother."

"Bloody hell man, get to it, or I'll toss you out and go back to bed."

Hunt drew himself up and stared at him. "You ruined an innocent woman last night."

Dante dropped his head into his hands. How the bloody hell had Hunt learned about him and Lydia so soon? Another reminder of why and how much he hated the Beau Monde.

"I did not ruin Miss Sanford."

"Were you caught in the dark kissing and fondling her?"

"No. We were kissing, but believe me, we didn't get near fondling, much to my regret."

Hunt growled, his fist drawn back.

Dante blocked him. "Don't try that again. That's the last time I'm saying it."

His brother straightened his jacket and pulled on his cuffs. "You will visit with Lord Sterling this morning and make your offer."

"Is that what you came here to do? Pretend I didn't know the proper thing to do when caught in a compromising situation with a proper young lady?"

Hunt leaned forward. "You have denounced marriage all your adult life. This is one time you cannot get away with it."

If the water pitcher sitting on his dresser had been full, he would have dumped the water on his pompous, arrogant brother's head. "What makes you think I intend to get away with anything? If you were so gleeful to hear gossip about me from last night, you missed the part where I announced my betrothal to Miss Sanford loud and clear. I intend to call on her father this morning. I will secure a special license and we shall be married post haste."

Hunt's jaw remained slack throughout Dante's rant. "You're serious."

Dante placed his hands on his hips. "Yes. I am serious."

His brother grinned. "I never thought I would see the day." He frowned and his face darkened. He pointed his finger at his brother. "Do not think you will continue with your conquests once you marry Miss Sanford. She is a lovely woman and deserves respect and faithfulness. Hell, she deserves more than you."

"Do you even know her?"

"No." Hunt waved his hand. "That is irrelevant. Any woman to whom you shackle yourself deserves better." Hunt looked around the room. "Where do you expect to house your wife? Certainly not in this dump."

"Your confidence in my common sense knows no bounds." Dante crossed his arms and leaned against the wall. "I will have to find a new place. A townhouse. Something not too far from the club."

"No. You need a better neighborhood than the club." Hunt walked to the door. "You will reside with Diana and me until you can find a proper place." He pointed at him as he opened the door. "I expect to receive an invitation to your wedding."

"Why? Are you afraid you will miss me surrendering and being shackled?"

"No." He opened the door and stepped out of the room. "I want to make sure you don't pack your bags and flee." The door slammed before Dante could throw a punch.

Dante dropped to the bed and rubbed his eyes with his fist. He probably shouldn't have been angry with Hunt's visit. His brother was correct. Dante had eschewed marriage for years. He'd had numerous mistresses and lovers.

But Lydia was different. Of course he would love taking her to bed. In her was a passionate woman waiting to be released. But it was more than that. He actually liked her, which was not something he generally felt for his conquests. He respected her intelligence and enjoyed her company.

Being older, she would not bore him to death with giggling and chattering. She knew her own mind and used it. In fact, the idea of the two of them butting heads over things in the coming years, and the making up that would follow was quite appealing.

He walked to his wardrobe and pulled out proper clothing to visit with an intended's father. He rang to have one of his landlady's employees bring him a bath. He looked around as he waited. Hunt was correct. This was a dump and Lydia deserved so much more.

LYDIA LAY flat on her back, staring at the canopy over her bed. She was to be married. To Dante Rose. Although she'd tried to talk him out of it last night, she knew in her heart it was not something she could dismiss.

She'd been a member of the *ton* long enough to know if she didn't marry Dante, she would be shunned. As he so rightly pointed out, what then would she do with her life? However, knowing that her life had only been comprised of social events and shopping was even more distressing.

She'd always held herself above the others because she had her occasional assignments with the Home Office. But they were few and far between since her only skill was languages, and that was not something they needed very much. As far as doing any sort of spy work, like Dante did, she'd always been dismissed as not being safe for a lady.

She rolled over and propped her chin on her fist. When she questioned him, Dante agreed to remain faithful providing she never banned him from her bed. That sounded reasonable, mostly because she had the feeling that the marriage bed with Dante would not be something for which she would need forbearance.

Now that her life was to go in a different direction than she'd imagined, it was time to consider what came next. Things she'd renounced years ago. A household of her own to manage, a husband in her bed, children. 'Twas the last one that made her smile.

She imagined a little boy with Dante's features and his charming personality. He would have all the female staff wrapped around his little finger. Perhaps they would have a daughter with the same traits. She frowned. They would have to keep an eye on that one.

Flipping over onto her back again, she smiled at the idea of this new life. The major surprise that had accompanied Dante's announcement of their betrothal had been her acceptance of it. Even though she came up with arguments against it, she was not unhappy with the turn of events. For some reason it felt right.

Especially since she'd received Dante's promise of fidelity. He might have been a rogue and a rake for years, but she knew him to be an honorable man. He would not promise what he had no intention of keeping.

A slight knock on her door drew her attention back to her surroundings. "Come."

Her maid, Alice, entered the room. "Good morning, Miss Sanford. Mr. Rose has arrived and is speaking with his lordship. He has requested that you meet with him in the drawing room when he is finished."

Lydia threw off the blanket and swung her legs over the edge of the bed. "Then I guess I better prepare for his visit."

She and Alice chatted as she helped her dress in a pale yellow linen dress with green embroidery on the cuffs and hem. It made her feel lighthearted. Or perhaps it was seeing Dante again.

Her betrothed.

As Alice brushed her hair, Lydia thought back to before Dante had entered the theater box the night before. That was when she had convinced herself that their relationship had come to an end. The devastation she'd felt when he entered and just stood there looking at her still brought tears to her eyes.

"I'm finished, miss. What do you think?" Alice smiled at her, and Lydia looked into the mirror. Her maid had fixed her hair in a twisted arrangement with tiny yellow and green flowers woven throughout.

"It looks lovely, Alice. Thank you so much." She stood and pulled on her white gloves and took one more look in the mirror. Yes, she looked fine enough to meet with her fiancé. She almost giggled like a young girl and immediately stopped herself.

She had no intention of being anything but the Lydia she'd always been. The Lydia Dante had known. Strong, intelligent, decisive, and most of all, not one to have her head turned by a handsome man.

Dante and marriage would not change that. Holding her head up, she left the room and made her way to the floor below to the drawing room. Once there, and realizing she hadn't yet broken her fast, she rang for tea to be sent up.

She had nibbled on toast and was on her second cup of tea

when the drawing room door was opened by one of the footmen and Dante entered.

Her heart immediately began to pound. He looked wonderful. His handsome face held a slight smile, and the look in his eyes as he studied her added a swarm of butterflies to her stomach.

"Miss Sanford." He bowed, then pushed back the hair that was perpetually falling forward.

She held her hand out. "Mr. Rose."

He took the steps to her slowly and deliberately. Her mouth went dry, and she ordered her heart to slow down, lest she swoon. She now faced a different Dante. Not the rake, not her partner in spying, not the man who turned her insides to mush. This man looked serious and in a small way, determined. "Good morning."

"Good morning to you, as well." She cleared her throat, hoping the words would come out without embarrassing herself. "Have you met with my father?"

He remained standing. "I have."

Before she could say anything else, he dropped to one knee and took her hand in his. "Last night was a debacle, sweetheart. Now I want to do this properly. I had never expected to be in this position, so I might do this all wrong." He stopped and took a deep breath. "Miss Sanford, will you grant me the honor of becoming my wife?"

Tears sprang to her eyes. She never expected this. She assumed with him making the announcement to all and sundry the night before and then pretty much ordering her to marry him, that this part was over. One more surprise from Mr. Dante Rose.

She reached out and cupped his cheek. "Yes, Mr. Rose. I will marry you."

With one quick tug, he pulled her down to the floor next to him and whipped out a beautiful diamond and sapphire ring from his pocket. She couldn't help but laugh at his antics as he placed it on her finger. Then he pulled her into his arms and kissed her in such a way that all she could think about was their upcoming wedding night.

* * *

"I THOUGHT a special license was supposed to grant you the right to marry early," Dante groused as he sat in Hunt's library sipping on a brandy.

"Stop complaining. Only one more day."

"And one more night," Dante said and scowled. "What I don't understand is why your wife is shielding Lydia like she's some sort of Buckingham Palace guard. Lydia and I haven't had a minute alone all week."

Hunt grinned. "Feeling a bit frustrated, little brother?" He stood and added more brandy to both of the crystal glass snifters they held.

"More than a little."

It had been two weeks since he and Lydia had been plunged into disgrace by the guardians of virtue of the Beau Monde. He'd spoken with her father the next morning, received the special license the day after, and then Diana and Amelia, Driscoll's wife, had descended upon him, swept Lydia away and began wedding preparations.

He'd only seen his fiancée in passing since then. Hunt and Diana had insisted on hosting the wedding breakfast and declared Dante was to give up his bachelor flat and move in with them while he looked for a decent place to bring his bride.

He was certain they were afraid he would sneak Lydia into his place and anticipate the vows as so many young couples did.

If only.

"Correct me if I'm wrong, brother, but if memory serves,

weren't you and your wife caught in a compromising situation that required a hasty wedding on your part?"

Looking both lofty and guilty at the same time—no easy feat—Hunt said, "That was a different matter."

Dante grinned at the pompous arse's discomfort. "And how is that?"

"It doesn't factor since we are speaking of your wedding." Hunt took a swallow of his brandy. "Do you love the girl, Dante?"

That brought him up short.

Did he love her? He desired her, most definitely. Did he like her? Yes. Did he enjoy her company? Few other people kept him as interested as Lydia did. But love? That meant an entirely different sort of commitment. One could marry and enjoy the pleasures of the marital bed, raise children and grow old, but love to him was something frightening. That would mean he'd have to admit to himself that there was one person in his life he could not get on without.

Hunt continued to stare at him. "I can see from your expression you're trying to talk yourself out of it." He stood and stretched. "Don't bother, I tried it myself and it doesn't work."

With those formidable words, Hunt downed the rest of his brandy, placed the glass on the table next to his chair and walked to the door. "Time for bed, little brother. You have a big day tomorrow."

DANTE TUGGED ONCE AGAIN on his neckcloth. Hunt's valet, who had insisted on helping him dress, although Dante had been dressing himself for years, had tied the damn thing too tight.

His brother, Driscoll stood next to him at the altar as they waited for the bride to arrive. He checked his timepiece for the tenth time. Or maybe eleventh, he'd lost count. "Is it some sort of custom to be late to one's own wedding?"

"Not if you're the groom. Then it's a scandal," Driscoll returned.

"How the devil do you know? You're no more a member of the Beau Monde than I am."

"Then why did you ask me?"

"Boredom."

Just then there was a rustle at the back of the church. The door had opened and Lydia's cousin, Marion, who was her bridesmaid, stepped through and turned to help Lydia enter.

All the blood rushed from his face to his feet. Thankfully it hadn't made a stop at his male member which would have been quite an embarrassment with a church full of people staring at him.

He took a deep breath. This was it. He was actually getting married. A day that in his mind had always brought on itchy skin. Instead, today it only brought him peace at finally seeing Lydia heading toward him, smiling brightly through her veil as she started down the aisle on her father's arm.

His bride wore a white satin gown, snug in the bodice and pulled tight around her stomach. The veil on her head covered her face and reached to the end of her gown. He had to smile because based on the Lydia he knew, he didn't think she chose the ensemble. She was far too practical for that. Most likely his brothers' wives pushed her into it.

Sterling handed his daughter over to him with a smile almost as bright as Lydia's. The man had been almost giddy during the marriage contract negotiations. He had apparently given up on ever seeing his daughter married and settled.

Instead of linking her arm to his, Dante took her hand and fingers clasped together, they faced the vicar.

The ceremony was long and boring. Dante wanted to get on with the service so they could have a quick breakfast and head for the hotel where he'd booked a room for three nights. He'd arranged with the hotel to have all their meals delivered to their door since he had no intention of letting Lydia out of the bed and warned his brother not to expect to see him at the club during that time. He'd even kept the hotel a secret.

Finally, they faced each other and spoke their vows. Dante took the ring from Driscoll and placed it on Lydia's finger. "With this ring I thee wed, with my body, I thee worship, and with all my worldly goods, I thee endow. In the name of the Father, the Son and the Holy Ghost. Amen."

They grinned at each other like a couple of urchins. Then, despite not knowing if it was allowed or not, Dante pulled up the veil covering his wife's face and tugged her into his arms and kissed her. Long and hard, until the vicar coughed, and several titters came from the those gathered in the church.

They turned and faced their guests and after a short visit to the office to sign the marriage book, made their way down the aisle to greet the attendees.

Dante smiled and shook hands all the time wondering how fast Lydia could eat her breakfast without becoming ill.

19

*L*ydia climbed into the carriage with Dante right behind her. He slammed the door and tapped on the ceiling to alert the driver. He slumped in his seat and sighed. "Thank God that's over with."

She raised her brows. "Dante, that was our wedding ceremony. I hope you weren't *too* bored. I supposed we could have made arrangements to make it more entertaining for you, so you wouldn't fall asleep." She hadn't intended for her words to come out quite so terse, but honestly, 'twas not promising that the first words one's new husband spoke when they were alone was to profess his relief that the wedding was over. Did he feel the same way about the marriage?

He immediately straightened. "Not at all." He paused. "I mean, yes, if I were to be honest, the wedding ceremony was a tad long. Didn't you think so?" He smiled his little boy, rakish smile. "Be honest."

Gad, she hated how he read her so easily. Of course it was long, boring, and truth be told she was glad it was over. But she would not start off their marriage by agreeing with everything he said. She sniffed and looked out the window. "It was longer than I expected."

Dante burst out laughing, reached over and pulled her onto his lap. At least she thought it was his lap. With so many layers of clothing on, it was genuinely hard to tell. He pushed the veil over her shoulder. "Are you even in there? With all this—" he waved his hand around "—clothing, I can barely feel you."

Drat, she had to agree with him again. This was not a good precedent to set. "Your sisters-in-law were a bit enthusiastic about having a proper wedding."

He smirked. "As opposed to having an improper one? That sounds like a great idea, why didn't we have one of those?"

"Dante, stop it." She couldn't help but laugh at his shenanigans.

"At least I can see your face. And lips." He stared hungrily at the spot he mentioned. Then, wrapping his arms around her he pulled her in for a kiss.

Good heavens, she thought the one in the church was scandalous, this one had her wanting to remove all the layers of their clothing and feel him skin-to-skin. Whatever was wrong with her?

She desired her husband, 'twas that simple.

He pulled back and nudging the veil away from her ear with his chin, he whispered. "Let's tell the driver to pass Hunt's house and go directly to the hotel."

She closed her eyes and sighed, tilting her head for better access. "What hotel?"

He kissed his way across her skin to her face, offering tiny kisses to her jaw, cheeks, and eyes. His lips brushed against hers as he spoke. "The hotel room I rented for three days for our honeymoon."

"All we get is three days?" she murmured.

"And nights." His lasts words were smothered on her lips and the hunger there sent shock waves through her entire body. "And if things go as planned, Mrs. Rose, we won't be able to walk after three days anyway."

Just as she thought she would melt into a puddle on the floor of the carriage, he pulled back and studied her as he moved his finger over her swollen lips. "Let's skip the breakfast. The only thing I'm hungry for is you."

"We can't do that." She placed her hands on his chest and moved him back. His strength, warmth and scent made it impossible to think straight. "Diana, and Driscoll's wife, Amelia, have gone to a great deal of work." She attempted to re-arrange herself, since it appeared they drew close to Hunt's townhouse.

Dante pushed her veil aside and kissed the back of her neck, nuzzling the space between her head and shoulder. She swatted at him. "Stop that. I need to look presentable."

"Presentable to me is naked and lying in bed."

She giggled and elbowed him. "If you don't behave yourself. . ."

"I never behave myself." He growled. "You love it, and it's too much fun not to."

The carriage came to a rolling stop and Dante sighed. "Can you at least eat fast?"

She turned and glared at him. "I expect you to be gracious and your usual charming self."

"I shall be so charming the ladies will be falling at my feet." He climbed out of the carriage and extended his hand.

Her eyes narrowed. "I have a hat pin in my reticule. I will use it if you are too charming to the female guests."

He grinned. "I was jesting." He touched her chin, his smile fading. "Those days are over, Lydia. I promised you. You are my wife and all I want. And need."

Her insides turned to mush, and she felt like telling the driver herself to head for the hotel. He looked sincere, but based on his life thus far, only time would tell if she could genuinely trust a rogue. Although she'd heard for years that reformed rakes made the best husbands.

But that was usually the case because they fell head over heels in love with their wives. As did Hunt and Driscoll, two other rogues. But Dante?

"Stop thinking so much, love. Let's get this breakfast over with, then off to the hotel."

* * *

IT HAD SEEMED numerous hours had passed before Dante had finally convinced Lydia that it was certainly proper for them to leave the breakfast and be on their way. They'd greeted the guests, mingled and chatted with glasses of champagne in hand, and eaten the lovely food Hunt's cook had prepared. Although he'd noticed Lydia barely ate, mostly pushing her food around on her plate.

Was she as anxious as he was to have this part of the day over? If so, most likely for different reasons than his. Despite her forward thinking, she was still a virgin and had to be a tad uneasy with what came after the little bit of intimacy they'd already shared. Although he hoped Diana had at least given her some idea of what to expect.

Toasts had been offered, as well as slaps on his back from Hunt, Driscoll and numerous friends. He'd listened to remarks about the parson's noose, leg-shackling, the end of life as he knew it. Thrown in were some comments not proper for ladies' ears.

He'd made his way over to his wife who had long ago shed her veil and her shoes. She waved her hand around as she spoke with her cousin, Marion. At his approach she looked up at him in a way that made him want to throw her over his shoulder and make his way out of the blasted house.

Now they were finally settled in the carriage on the way to

the hotel. Attempting to keep himself under control until they reached their destination, he took her hand in his. "Did you enjoy the breakfast?"

She leaned back on the squab and sighed. "Yes, it was lovely."

"But long."

She attempted to look cross, but a smile broke out. "Yes. Long. Just like our wedding ceremony."

Lydia smoothed out the wrinkles in her gown. "We spent so little time together the past two weeks, I'm not even sure where we will live when we return from the hotel."

He was listening to his wife he assured himself, but he wanted nothing more than to kiss her. It was probably a better idea to keep his hands off her until they reached their destination. Stripping his new bride bare and relieving her of her maidenhead in a moving carriage would not be the most gentlemanly thing he'd ever done. Unfortunately, it would not be the worst thing he'd ever done with a woman, either.

However, this was not just a woman, but his wife who deserved his respect and not to be treated like one if his light-skirts. He shook his head, still trying to adjust to the *wife* moniker.

In answer to her question, he said, "I have looked at a few townhouses to lease. Until we find something, we will be residing with Hunt and Diana. My pompous, arrogant brother referred to my bachelor flat as a dump."

"Is it?"

He thought for a minute. "Yes. I suppose it is."

She laughed and he joined her. "Do I get to be part of the decision on where we live?"

Staring in her eyes, Dante raised her hand, tugged her glove off one finger at a time, and kissed the soft skin on her wrist. "Of course. That is why I have only looked at a few possibilities."

Lydia shivered and he thanked God the carriage stopped. He looked up. "We're here."

He loved watching his wife's flushed face, and before the hotel footman could make it to the carriage, Dante opened the door and hopped out.

She took his hand and stepped down. "I should have changed before we left Hunt's house. I look silly walking into the hotel in a wedding gown."

He took her arm and moved her forward. "You would look silly if you were coming from a garden party, but you are arriving from your wedding. Besides, the hotel knows we're recently married."

"How would they know?"

He whisked her through the front door, held open by an impressive looking footman. "Because I rented the bridal suite and asked for all our meals to be brought to our room."

She gasped and drew back. "You didn't!"

"I did." He loved her outrage. Perhaps he could keep her annoyed with him until they made it to bed. Then he would enjoy turning all that anger into passion.

They checked in, and one of the footmen directed them to their suite on the upper floor. It was a spacious room, well appointed in pale rose and green wallpaper. A very large, very tempting bed took up a good part of the room, covered in a deeper rose and green counterpane.

The carpet under their feet was plush enough to sleep on. Dante did a quick survey of the room, noting all the places where they could make love. Yes, this would be a wonderful honeymoon.

Lydia looked nervous. He had to remember he was used to experienced women, but it was his job as her husband to make sure she was relaxed enough to enjoy her first time and look forward to more of his attentions. "Once our bags arrive, you will want to change into something more comfortable."

She nodded and licked her lips. He sauntered up to her and she backed up a step. He reached out and pulled her to him, wrapping his arms around her waist, but keeping a little bit of distance between them. "Relax, sweeting. I have no intention of pouncing on you."

"I didn't think that." Her bravado was amusing, but he would never let her know that. Before he could comment on it, a slight knock on the door drew their attention.

Dante opened the door and allowed the footman to bring in their bags. Once they were placed where Lydia wanted them, he gave him a few coins and he left.

He remained near the door, which seemed to please Lydia. "I noticed a bar downstairs. I think I will have a drink or two and give you some privacy to change."

She slumped in relief. "Thank you."

He nodded and left. Where the blasted hell was the independent, spirited, passionate woman he'd spent the last few weeks with? Did all new brides act this way on their wedding night?

Patience, Dante. She needs time.

* * *

LYDIA HAD MADE use of the lovely bathing room attached to their suite, feeling refreshed after the long day, and wearing all those clothes. There were times during the day she felt as though she couldn't breathe with the layers of garments her new sisters-in-law insisted she must wear to be a proper bride.

The hotel had provided small jars of sweet-smelling soap and soft drying cloths for her use. She decided not to wash her hair since she didn't have time to dry it before the fire that burned in the fireplace.

Now she sat in the room, fidgeting while she awaited Dante's return. About ten minutes before a maid had arrived and after ascertaining she was properly attired, waved a footman in who carried a stand with ice and a champagne bottle. They also set out an array of small sandwiches and cakes. After a slight bow, they both left.

Properly attired, indeed. She wore a nightgown the ladies had insisted she must have for her wedding night. For goodness sake, it was practically transparent. However, it came with a white silk dressing gown that covered her quite nicely.

SHE JERKED when the door opened, and Dante entered. He looked her up and down with such hunger, she almost fled the room. He shook his head slightly. "You look beautiful, Lydia." He walked toward her slowly, and instead of feeling as though she wanted to back up, she moved toward him. Her insides had melted just having him in the room.

They reached each other and he unhurriedly raised his hand and moved aside a lock of hair that had fallen over her eye. "I've never seen you with your hair down."

She had no idea what to say, so she licked her dry lips. His warm hand took her face and held it gently. "I've waited a long time for this."

Attempting to make light of the growing serious situation, she grinned. "I doubt you went long without this."

"Ah, not so, my love. I have not touched another woman since the moment I walked into Sir Phillip's office all those weeks ago."

She smirked.

"'Tis true." He traced her features with his finger. "No other woman has appealed to me since I met you."

Why did she believe him? Perhaps it was the look in his eyes and the fact that she had learned so much about this man who stood before her. He was a rake, a rogue, and a libertine, but he was also an honest and honorable man. He was protective, caring. And her husband.

He swept her, weightless, into his arms and kissed her with all the longing she felt herself. Instead of taking her to the bed which she thought he would do, he walked to the fireplace and placed her on the settee in front of the low flame.

He straightened. "I see they brought the champagne I ordered." Dante picked up the bottle, opened it and poured the sparkling liquid into two thin glasses. Walking to her, he handed her one. "I would prefer to get out of these clothes. Is that all right with you?"

She sipped the drink. "Yes." She looked around frantically. "Where will you change?"

"Relax, my love. I will avail myself of the bathing room." He bent over and gave her a quick, light kiss. "Don't go anywhere."

He grabbed his banyan and whistling a soft tune, left the room.

Lydia took a deep breath and placed the glass on the table. It was nice to feel relaxed, but she didn't want to drink too much. As nervous as she was, it was important to be aware of what was going on.

Within a record amount of time, Dante returned from the bathing room, wearing a red and black striped dressing gown. Since his hair was damp, it appeared he took the quickest bath in history. As he walked toward her, she caught a glimpse of his bare leg and the muscles in her stomach twisted.

He sat alongside her, resting his arm along the back of the settee, playing with the ends of her hair. "I want you to know that as much as I look forward to this, I will be gentle. I will not hurt you or embarrass you. Ever."

She nodded. "I know that. I trust you."

As though that was a cue for them to begin, he downed the champagne from his glass, and shifted closer to her and took her in his arms. "That means more to me than anything you could have said."

Putting a large hand to her waist, he drew her closer. His head bent, and oh so gently, pressed his lips to hers. He brushed them back and forth, then with a slight groan, crushed her to him.

His slow drugging kiss worked to relax her more than all the champagne in the world. He nudged her lips with his tongue, and she granted him entrance, shocked at her reaction to him as he swept into her mouth, tasting, touching, sucking.

She fought him, tongue for tongue. He pulled back and leaned his forehead against hers. "I suggest we move this activity to the bed." They were both panting, and Lydia felt the need to remove her dressing gown, even if the nightgown underneath was invisible.

"Yes. I think you are right."

Once again he scooped her into his arms, kissing her all the way to the bed where he gently laid her down. "Remove your dressing gown," he whispered.

She looked him in the eyes and realized she wanted to do that. Very much. Slowly, she pulled the garment off and tossed it to the floor.

His eyes grew wide, and he looked her up and down. "Dear God, you're exquisite." He climbed in next to her. "And all mine."

Another possessive, hungry kiss had her pushing the banyan off his shoulders, running her hands over his smooth muscles. Dante flicked his fingers and untied the garment. She pushed it all the way off and he gathered it up and tossed it on top of her dressing gown. Her nipples hardened at his stare. "I love this nightgown, and want you to wear it many times, but right now I want it off."

He slid it over her shoulders, down her body to her feet

where it also landed on the pile of discarded clothes. He urged her down so they were lying face-to-face.

She inhaled deeply as his hand wandered her body, studying her as if she were a precious possession, stopping to squeeze, caress, and fondle. His ardor was surprisingly, touchingly, restrained.

* * *

DANTE DIPPED his head to take one turgid nipple into his mouth. He licked, encircling the teasing bud with his tongue. Lydia let out a soft moan.

"DO YOU LIKE THAT?"

"Hmmm."

"I'll take that as a yes." He grinned and continued his ministrations. "We've only just started, love." His tongue made a path down her ribs to her stomach. She shifted her legs, tossing her head back and forth with growing need.

Rather than shock her right from the start, he moved back up and kissed her while his hands and fingers kept busy stroking her curves, with feathering touches that had her panting.

Everything in his being was focused on the beautiful woman lying alongside him. He curled his arm around her shoulders and pulled her toward him, running circles over the bare skin of her shoulders and back, moving down, cupping her lush bottom. He pulled her against his erection, rubbing gently, closing his eyes at the feel of her naked skin against his. The moment he'd been dreaming about for weeks.

His hand slid over her hip, heading for the dark curls at the juncture of her thighs. His fingers found her wet center. He circled, pressed and circled again.

Lydia sucked in a deep breath. "Yesss. Oh, that is perfect. Don't stop."

Not one for conversation during lovemaking, he thought perhaps this being his wife's first time, a few love words and compliments might be in order.

He whispered in her ear while sucking on her earlobe, telling her how much he desired her, how beautiful she was. He was amazed to find it stimulating for himself. 'Twas nice to be doing something new and different with his wife.

It might have been the words he whispered, or just Lydia's growing enthusiasm, but she slowly moved her hand from where it had rested on his chest, growing closer to his cock. Taking her hand, he guided it to himself. "Yes, sweetheart. Touch me."

"It feels so odd." She gave a soft laugh. "Probably not to you."

He couldn't help it, he laughed. Something else he'd never done during lovemaking. It was freeing. He didn't feel the usual pressure to perform, to live up to the reputation he'd developed. And not just because it was his wife's first time. In some ways he felt as though it was the first *real* time for him. As if all his previous encounters had been practice.

"Ah, Lydia, love." He squeezed her shoulder and continued to thumb her center where he knew she would find the most pleasure. She was growing braver with her handling his cock. "That's it, move your hand up and down." He gritted his teeth. "Yes. Just like that."

His wife was a fast learner. Her breathing increased and he felt her heart pounding against his chest. From her frantic movements and breathing, it was apparent she was nearing a climax.

"Dante, I need something. I feel very strange, as if something was missing."

"Relax, sweetheart. Don't strain. It will come."

"What?"

He smiled against her mouth. "You'll see." Not shifting his fingers, he moved his mouth over hers and kissed her with all the passion he'd been tamping down for weeks.

"Yes. I can feel something. I think—" She stiffened and pressed against his hand, a low moan coming from her mouth.

She was exquisite in her passion. The muscles in her face seemed to melt, as did the rest of her body. "Oh, my. That is. That is. . ." She lay panting, her chest heaving, looking at him with wonder.

"Yes, my love. I know." He shifted so he covered her body with his. Leaning on his elbows, he cupped her face. "This will hurt, but only for an instant. We will take it slow."

She studied him with glazed eyes. "All right."

It was probably the best time to get the pain over with since she seemed a tad unfocused. He edged his cock into her entrance, sliding in with ease until he met the female obstruction. He gripped her hands and placed their linked fingers above her head. He leaned down and kissed her as he thrust forward.

Lydia squeaked a short yelp, her eyes opening wide. His tongue plunged into her mouth as he continued to kiss her but kept his body still. Once he felt her tensed muscles relax, he pulled out and then back in again, starting the dance of lovers from the beginning of time.

It didn't take her long to begin moving again, alerting him to her increasing hunger for another release. It had been so long he wasn't certain he could last until she broke apart again, but this was his wife. This was her first time. He would make it good for her no matter how hard it was for him.

Within minutes she moaned again and he felt her muscles grip him as he gave a few final thrusts and then spilled his seed into her body. Making her his.

Forever.

hen Dante had told her that they would spend their entire honeymoon in bed, Lydia had laughed. However, it turned out he hadn't been joking, and they truly did not put on a stitch of clothing for three solid days. 'Twas too bad she'd spent so much time choosing what to pack for their trip.

They made love in bed, ate their meals in bed, read to each other in bed, played cards and chess in bed—Dante had thought of everything—and talked about their lives up to the point where they'd met, in bed. They did manage to get out of the bed to take a few baths, but they did it together and ended up making a mess on the floor each time since Dante thought the warm water of the bath would be great for making love.

He paid the maid the first day she came to clean the room to not come back until they checked out. Lydia had been almost embarrassed to leave the hotel, sure all the staff were talking about them.

But it had been, without a doubt, the best three days of her life.

They sat next to each other, holding hands as the carriage

pulled away from the hotel and headed to Hunt's townhouse. Despite their rigorous activities, Lydia felt anything but tired. A tad sore, perhaps, but otherwise she was ready to begin her new life.

"Do you have more residences for us to look at as a potential lease?"

Dante squeezed her hand. "No. Only those few I've already looked at. How do you feel about living in London all year? Because of the Rose Room, I need to stay in Town." He shifted to look at her. "I know you left every year to either visit friends or reside at your father's estate in the country."

She gave his question some thought. London was a horrible place to be in the summertime when the smells and heat could choke one. "I guess I never gave it much thought, since it was something I did automatically. But it doesn't matter since it's necessary for us to say here."

"I could purchase a small estate in the country that you could retire to each summer."

Alarm bells went off in her head and the deep feeling of contentment slowly faded. Did he want her out of London so he could return to his rakish ways? Would he be willing to spend the money on a house he would never visit? Just to keep her out of the way?

"What are you thinking, my love? You look upset."

"Nothing." She attempted a smile. She would never tell him her thoughts. They'd made love numerous times but he never once uttered the words she wanted to hear. A married man never visited other women's beds if he loved his wife. Did he love her?

She hated to think about becoming a jealous suspicious wife, but her confidence had dipped just a tad. She shrugged her shoulders. "It matters not if I stay in London. Perhaps it's not as bad as I've heard."

Once the words left her mouth she studied him carefully. Did he look disappointed? Annoyed?

She had to stop this craziness, because that's what it was. Then her mind continued to torture her. Dante spent time around other women by merely working in the club. And not the best sort of women, either. And what about all his past lovers? Wouldn't they expect him to resume his old ways since many married men continued to maintain a mistress?

The lovely breakfast they'd eaten before leaving the hotel threatened to make a re-appearance on her shoes. Once again she told herself this entire line of thinking was ridiculous and she had to turn her thoughts from it.

"I would like to continue working at the club." Now where had that statement come from? Was it because she wanted a sense of contributing, or was she hoping to keep an eye on her husband?

"No."

She stiffened, suspicion raising its ugly head again. "Why not?"

"Now that I am back to work, Driscoll can return to his duties, and we won't need you."

She felt as though he'd slapped her in the face. He couldn't have said anything worse. *We don't need you.* Like in *I don't need you?*

She turned her head to look out the window, the quickly appearing tears she refused to release almost choking her.

"Lydia?" Dante placed his finger under her chin and turned her head toward him.

Oh, God, please don't let these tears fall. "Wh__" She cleared her throat of the frog that had taken up residence. "What?"

"Something is troubling you."

She tightened her lips and shook her head. And to her dismay one tear dripped down her face. Angrily, she swiped it away. Mad at him, mad at herself and mostly mad at what a cake she was making of herself. Another tear broke loose. She drew in a shuddering breath, and then the floodgates opened.

Dante drew her into his arms and rested his chin on her head. "What's wrong, Lydia? Is it working at the club? If you feel that strongly about it, perhaps you could work on the books again. Driscoll could probably use a night off on a regular basis."

She pulled back, wiping her cheeks. "Truly?"

"Sweetheart, if it means that much to you, then yes. As long as you do not wander the game floor."

She looked into his eyes and only saw caring, and maybe even a bit of love. Her heart already belonged to him. That she'd known when she had awaited him at the Ambassador's theater box, expecting to say goodbye. "Yes. I agree." There she went, agreeing with him again.

"I must visit the club tonight, to at least see how things are going, and to assure my brother that I am alive and well, and my wife didn't wear me out."

She grinned, feeling much better at his light words. "I will go with you."

He hesitated at first, but then said, "Of course."

The ride went quickly after that, and soon they were rolling to a stop in front of Hunt's home. The driver jumped down and opened the door, allowing Dante to step out and extend his hand to her.

The front door opened and a footman stepped out. "Good morning, Mr. Rose." He beamed in Lydia's direction. "And good morning to you as well, Mrs. Rose."

It felt odd to be addressed that way but felt wonderful at the same time. "Thank you."

They stepped through the door and Diana came hustling down the stairs. "There you are. We were expecting you for breakfast."

Dante accepted Diana's hug. She turned to Lydia. "My new sister-in-law!" She linked her arm into Lydia's and they started up the stairs. "You must tell me all about your trip. Did you see any sights?"

Lydia turned back to Dante who was following them up the stairs and they both burst into laughter.

"Oh, my. That probably wasn't a smart question now, was it?" Diana raised her hands to her face, attempting to hide her blush.

* * *

"Welcome back, boss." Keniel was the first to greet them as Dante and Lydia entered the club from the back door.

"Good evening, Mrs. Rose." Keniel took her extended hand and kissed it. "Are you here to keep the players at the *vingt-et-un* table enchanted with your presence?"

"No!" Dante blurted out the word before even thinking. First, he wasn't too happy with all the charm oozing from his manager and directed at his wife, and second to suggest she deal cards was enough to have him gritting his teeth.

"Mrs. Rose will be working on the books up in the office."

"Ah." Keniel stepped back and his entire demeanor changed. "I am sure Driscoll will be grateful for the help." He nodded and walked toward the employees' room.

Lydia turned on him the minute Keniel was out of sight. "That was quite rude, Dante."

"What?" He was already feeling guilty at his abrupt behavior with his manager, but he'd had an overwhelming sense of guarding what was his that he'd never felt before. And probably had scoffed at his brothers for doing the same thing with their wives.

"He was only asking a question, and considering I've dealt before, it wasn't an unreasonable one." They started up the stairs to the level where the office and dining room were located.

"No dealing."

Lydia sighed. "I know that."

They entered the dining room and Dante immediately poured himself a cup of coffee. It was too early for dinner to be served, which was usually brought up from the kitchen and left as a buffet for him and Driscoll. They had invited Keniel to join them more than once, but he'd always declined.

Tonight he was glad he had.

"Dante, this message came for you a few days ago. I told Driscoll about it, but he said to hold onto it until you returned." Daniels, one of his security guards held out a folded piece of paper.

"Thank you." Dante took the missive and opened it as the security guard left. He glanced at the terse words.

I need to speak with you and Miss Sanford. Please attend me as soon as possible.

Sir Phillip

He looked up at Lydia. "It seems we are being summoned by Sir Phillip."

Lydia removed the paper from his hand and studied it. "He apparently isn't aware of our marriage." She glanced up at him. "Maybe he needs to get statements from us."

"I already gave them one when you were busy making wedding plans." The summons then had also been curt. He'd met with Sir Phillip and told him what he'd seen the night the Ambassador had been confronted. Another man had been present in the office at the time who Dante had never seen before. A small, quiet sort who Dante thought looked like a squirrel as he scribbled away. The man took notes and then handed the paper to him which Dante read over and signed. At the time it appeared his part of the investigation was over.

"I didn't know you had already met with Sir Phillip."

"He didn't ask in his summons to have you present as well, so with you so busy with Diana and Amelia, it slipped my mind."

Lydia studied the note again. "Yet now he wants to see both of us." She shrugged and dropped the missive on the table. "I guess we will find out soon enough."

THE NEXT MORNING, Dante and Lydia left Hunt's townhouse and climbed into his carriage for the trip to Sir Phillip's office. They were both silent, having enjoyed meager sleep the night before. Once they'd returned from the club and climbed into bed, they reached for each other, sleep far from their minds.

Dante had been thrilled at how receptive Lydia was to his attentions. She'd turned out to be an enthusiastic bed partner, willing to try things he'd never expected a woman of her station to indulge in. Although he'd had his share of ladies of the *ton* in his bed, they had always been widows, not young innocent women.

Yes, this marriage would not be the boring, insipid relationship he'd always assumed marriage would be.

Lydia sat with her head resting on the soft leather squab, her eyes closed. She was perfection. Smooth, soft skin, features that were not perfect, but lent a bit of interest to her face. But the best part of his wife, aside from how she'd embraced the marriage bed, was how much he enjoyed her company. The numerous women he'd bedded over the years had been for only one purpose. He'd found it exciting that in between making love during their three day trip, they'd discussed numerous subjects.

He'd confirmed what he'd always thought. Lydia was an intelligent woman with a soft, caring side. Who would have known he, the sworn bachelor, would step willingly into the parson's noose and then enjoy every moment? Life certainly had a way of moving one in a direction never anticipated.

Sir Phillip greeted them at the door and led them to his office. 'Twas hard to read the man since he had the ability to keep a straight face, showing no emotion no matter the situation.

"Felicitations on your marriage," Sir Phillip said as he took his seat behind the desk and waved at the two chairs in front of him for them to sit.

"Thank you," they said together.

The man actually smiled at them which was quite a surprise. "I didn't know about the happy event until I sent the note to you and Driscoll was kind enough to send a message back that you were on your honeymoon." He shook his head. "Very few things in life take me by surprise, but I admit this was one of them."

He cleared his throat and leaned forward. "I have news about the Ambassador and your investigation of which you must be made aware."

Dante glanced at Lydia, who raised her eyebrows in question.

"First of all, I congratulate you both on a job well done. The Ambassador was quite cooperative in naming the source of his information." He stopped and seemed to give himself time to consider his words.

"The woman in question was mistress to one of our Home Office high ranking officials."

This was news to Dante since when he'd appeared before Sir Phillip the last time, he was given no information, but was merely asked to give a statement.

"That is how she got the information she passed to the Ambassador?" Lydia asked.

"Yes. She and the Ambassador were both confronted that night at the theater. As was the usual procedure, the Ambassador had diplomatic immunity from prosecution and could be detained, but not arrested."

"I have a feeling there is more to the story. What is it you are not telling us, since this all seems to be normal protocol?"

Sir Phillip took a deep breath and stared at him. "The woman involved with the Ambassador was of course, arrested, as well as her contact at the Home Office. However, I received word the morning I sent the note that the Ambassador has not returned to Germany."

Dante frowned. "Isn't that the usual process when a high-ranking embassy official is involved in espionage?"

"Yes. But, at this time I am unable to get any information as to how and why he remains in England."

Since Sir Phillip had a web of contacts that was certainly a surprise.

Sir Phillip paused for a moment, gathering his words. "I just learned yesterday that the woman in question was found dead in her cell in gaol."

Dante and Lydia looked at each other. Dante reached for her hand. Sir Phillip continued. "Poisoned. No one is sure how she got the deadly drug. Then the man from the Home Office has also met with an unfortunate accident while under house arrest."

"Dead?" Dante asked.

"Yes." Sir Phillip stared at Dante. "That is why I called you both here today. I believe there is a possibility that you and your wife might be in danger."

"*Y*ou are to go nowhere without me." Dante set down that edict the moment they settled into the carriage for their return trip home.

Lydia wanted to argue against his arrogance, but she was too frightened to do so. She had no intention of going anywhere without him. Her assignments with the Home Office had never been dangerous because translating languages didn't exactly lead to murder.

Until now.

"We can't live in fear the rest of our lives." She tried in vain to stop her voice from shaking. "We have to find out who killed those two people and have them arrested and charged."

Dante pointed his finger at her. "*You* will do nothing to find out who killed those people. *I* will visit with the Metropolitan Police first and then with whatever information I receive, hire an investigator to find the murderer for us."

Sir Phillip had given them the names of the guards at the gaol who were responsible for the Home Office man's mistress who'd been murdered, and the name and address of the traitor himself who'd been under house arrest. Sir Phillip had been reluctant to surrender the information, but when Dante had threatened to blow the whistle on the entire secret operation run by Sir Phillip, the man had relented.

Currently, Dante held the crumbled piece of paper with the names on it in his hand. "After some consideration, I believe the best place for me to start is probably not at the police department. Since this operation, like all of them with Sir Phillip, was surreptitious, he would have been unable to offer the information necessary to convince the police that the deaths were not accidents. Hence I doubt I would get any cooperation from them. What I will do is take a trip to Bath and visit with Mr. Nick Smith."

Lydia frowned. "Who is he?"

"A former mudlark and cut-purse, raised in the East End of London, who rose above it all to own an extremely profitable and exclusive gaming club in Bath. From what I've heard he married the sister of an Earl—if you could believe it—and sold the gambling club. He is now the owner of numerous businesses and is an upstanding member of Bath society."

"He sounds like an amazing man. But why contact him?"

"Because he's kept his contacts and knows every criminal in London, as well as Bath, and can ferret out information for us faster than the entire Metropolitan Police Department."

"How do you know him?"

"When Driscoll and I decided to start up a gaming club ourselves and Hunt agreed to finance it as a silent partner, we asked around and learned about Nick. We spent a couple of days with him, and he gave us great advice and helped to get our club up and running."

"I shall go with you when you see Mr. Smith." Until this was settled, she had no intention of letting him out of her sight.

He didn't need time to answer that request, it seemed, since he immediately agreed. "I don't want you in London with me in Bath. We'll take the train and a hackney from the railway station to Smith's house."

She grinned. "You are so sure of his welcome?"

"Yes. He's a friendly, open fellow. He owns two hotels so we will stay in one of them."

Even though they were traveling to Bath to attempt to keep themselves from being murdered, she was excited by the trip. "I've only been in Bath a few times, but it has been years. I'd forgotten how much I like it."

The carriage drew up to Hunt's townhouse. "When will we go?"

Dante looked at his timepiece. "I believe there is a train to Bath at four-thirty."

Her jaw dropped. "You mean to go right away. Now?"

He opened the door and turned to help her out. "There is no better time than now. I refuse to live under a threat; and getting us both out of London right now is a good idea."

"What about the club?"

He took her arm and moved her forward. "It survived for the past few weeks while we were working on the assignment. It will do just fine with me gone again. Besides, Keniel can take over a lot of my duties like he did before."

They walked up the steps to the house, the door opening before they reached the top. They greeted the butler and continued up the stairs to the drawing room.

"You two were off early today." Diana spoke softly as she sat on the sofa with the Huntingtons' pride and joy and heir, Master George Hanover Rose, settled on her lap, sound asleep.

"We had business with Sir Phillip. Is Hunt around?" Dante asked.

"Yes. I believe he's in the library. Have you broken your fast?" She continued to speak in a low voice.

Lydia nodded. "Yes, but a cup of tea would be wonderful right now."

Diana gestured with her head to the bell pull alongside the door and began to rise. "Ring for some. I could use a cup myself. I'm going to put the little one down for his nap."

As Lydia moved to the door, Dante strode up to her. "I will be in the library with Hunt." He wrapped his arm around her shoulders and pulled her close. "Remember, don't leave the house."

She nodded her consent and he kissed her on the forehead and left.

Lydia walked around the room, waiting for a footman to appear. She rubbed her hands up and down her arms, trying to warm herself. A foolish endeavor since she was not cold from the air, but from the fear that someone might be out there waiting for the opportunity to kill her and Dante.

DANTE STROLLED into the library to see Hunt bent over the desk shuffling papers around. "Don't you employ a man to do that for you? Where is your secretary?"

Hunt looked up and smiled. He stretched and then leaned back in his oversized chair that had belonged to their father, and most likely the fathers before him for a few generations. "What did Sir Phillip want?"

Since all three brothers did occasional work for the Crown, they knew about each other's assignments unless they were told to keep it to themselves as a top priority matter.

"The German Ambassador is still in London."

Hunt frowned. "Why? I thought he would have been sent back to Germany by now."

"I thought so, too. It's been three weeks since he was detained at the theater."

"I wonder how long these things take." Hunt said.

Dante pulled out the chair in front of his brother's desk and sat. "That's not the worst of it." He paused. "It seems that the two other people involved, the woman who was passing the secrets to the Ambassador and the man in the Home Office she was mistress to and getting the information from, have both turned up dead. Even though the woman was in gaol at the time and the man under house arrest in his own home."

Hunt let out a long, low whistle. Then he sat up and stared at him. "What about you and Lydia? Are you in danger?"

Dante nodded. "Sir Phillip seems to think that's a possibility. He warned us to be aware of the potential threat."

"You will go to my estate in the country. I'll send two footmen with you."

Dante held up his hand. "No. We must get this solved. Sir Phillip's hands are tied because he can't reveal his involvement in all this. The Metropolitan Police have deemed them accidents."

Hunt stood and paced. "This is unacceptable. Sir Phillip and his secrets got you and Lydia involved in this. He cannot just drop the ball and tell you to be careful. He should be the one investigating."

"Not if he is to retain his covert operation."

"Blast his covert operation!" Hunt pinched the bridge of his nose with his thumb and forefinger and took a deep breath. "All right. I don't like it, but I understand. So what is your plan? Hire an investigator?"

Dante ran his fingers through his hair. "My first thought was Nick Smith."

"Ah. The notorious Nick Smith. I thought he gave up all his underground activities when he sold his club?"

"He did. But he's maintained his contacts. I still hear about him at times. His name is bandied about occasionally in the Rose Room."

Hunt returned to his seat and leaned back, crossing his arms over his chest. "Do you want my carriage? I think it's more comfortable than yours for long distance travel."

"Thank you, but no. We will be taking the train this afternoon. I want to get Lydia out of London as quickly as possible."

Hunt nodded. "Good idea. What can I do to help?"

Dante stood. "My absence at the club has hurt Driscoll, and now I'll be gone again. Hopefully only for a day or two. If you could give some assistance there, it would be a huge help."

"Done."

Hunt and Dante made their way from the library to the drawing room where tea was just being served. Although he was anxious to be on his way, it was a few hours until the train left, so he decided to curb his unease and let his wife enjoy her tea before they needed to pack.

The four of them chatted for a while, with a definite pall over the group. Apparently Lydia must have told Diana about the meeting with Sir Phillip because she kept looking back and forth between the two of them with concern. "Are you sure it wouldn't be better to stay here and hire someone to find whoever is behind the two deaths?"

"I can't just sit still, Diana. Someone is out there ready to cause harm to Lydia and me. Even if Nick can't come up with some suggestions as to who might be involved in this, he can certainly recommend someone to act as a guard for my wife."

"Me?" Lydia said as she held her teacup close to her mouth. "What about you? Are you invincible?"

"I'm a man. I can take care of myself."

She put her teacup down with a bang. "So was the man from the Home Office, who was in his own home, and he was murdered."

"She's right, you know, Dante," Diana said. "If someone wants you dead it matters not if you're a man or a woman."

He waved them off. "I am going upstairs to pack for the

next few days." He turned to Lydia. "When you're finished with your tea, I suggest you do the same." He checked his timepiece. "The train leaves in three hours and I need to stop at the club first to speak with Driscoll and Keniel."

He left the room and bounded up the stairs. It took him less than thirty minutes to pack everything he would need. He still hadn't employed a valet, which was something he still fought against. He didn't need to hire someone to tie his ascot or pull off his boots. Clothing that needed attention was sent out to a laundry near the club who also employed a seamstress.

Lydia, however had brought a lady's maid with her when she had left her father's home. Since he hadn't wanted anyone else with them for their honeymoon, he'd given the maid the time off, with pay, and acted as lady's maid to his wife. Except there had only been one occasion to help her dress and that was when they were leaving the hotel to return home. He grinned at the thought.

Just as he was snapping his bag closed, Lydia entered their bedchamber. "I see you're ready to go. Just give me another half hour?"

"Yes. I already told your maid, I forget her name—"

"—Alice."

"Right. I already instructed her to start packing for a couple of days."

"Thank you. I will be as quick as possible because I know you want to stop at the club first." She sped to her dressing room where her maid was folding dresses and placing them into a trunk. Dante picked up his satchel and headed downstairs.

He found Hunt still in the library. Dante walked over to the sideboard and poured a brandy and held up the bottle to his brother.

"Yes. I'll take one. Only two fingers. I still have work to do."

They sipped their drinks in light conversation since Dante

didn't care to dwell too much on what he and Lydia could possibly be facing. He checked his timepiece three times before Lydia entered the library, pulling on her gloves. "I'm ready."

Dante downed the rest of his drink and placed the glass back on the sideboard. "Then let us be off." He took her elbow and turned back to Hunt. "We shall be no more than a couple of days."

Hunt nodded. "Good luck. I hope Smith can help you. You are taking footmen with you?"

"I have one, Lyons, plus the driver. I'm sure we'll be fine."

"Are they carrying pistols?"

"Yes."

After a hug from Diana at the door, they left the house and entered the carriage, Lyons riding on the back of the vehicle.

The first stop at the club went well. He and Lydia both went up to the office where he talked to Driscoll and Keniel. They assured him all would be well while he was gone. They still had an hour before the train would leave, so some of Dante's anxiety eased as they said their goodbyes and climbed back into the carriage.

They started off for the train and immediately hit traffic. "It's a good thing we allowed enough time. This is the last train to Bath today." He tried to avoid the growing uneasiness at being stuck in a traffic snarl.

The vehicle crawled along until with only twenty minutes left to spare they arrived at Paddington Station. Once they were inside the station, he said, "I will purchase the tickets. Stay with Lyons and the bags; I'll send a porter over to collect them. Then meet me at the platform." Dante gave her a quick kiss on the cheek and headed to the ticket counter.

As oftentimes happened in life, the line was long and moved slowly. Dante kept checking his timepiece. Finally, he was able to purchase their tickets and headed back to the platform.

Growing frantic, he reached the point where he pushed people aside so he could move along.

He spotted Lydia who waved at him. He slumped with relief and continued toward her a few moments before she screamed and disappeared, the throng surrounding her swallowing her up.

---

*D*ante's heart came to an abrupt halt, then started up with a vengeance when he heard Lydia scream. He raced forward, shoving people out of the way, knocking one gentleman to the ground, but kept going. As he reached the crowd huddled around her, his eyes flicked to a man racing away, looking back over his shoulder.

Dante screamed and gestured toward the man. "Lyons, go stop that man."

He dropped to his knees and looked at his wife. She lay on her side, pale, with blood seeping on the ground from underneath her. "Lydia." He placed his hand under her shoulders and gently pulled her forward. She groaned, and he was never so glad to hear that sound. At least she wasn't dead.

He looked up. "Please move back so I can attend my wife. Will someone summon a hackney?"

"I will, sir." A lad of about fifteen years spoke up.

"Thank you."

Dante winced as he looked over her shoulder to see a large knife sticking out of her back, blood seeping from the wound. He felt his own blood leave his face and settle somewhere near his feet. He knew better than to try to remove the weapon since that would increase the blood flow. "Sweetheart, can you hear me?"

Lydia's eyelids flicked open and she licked her lips. "Yes. I have a terrible pain in my back."

Thinking it was not a good idea to tell her about the knife, he eased her close to him and spoke into her ear. "You've been injured. I'm taking you to hospital."

Just then a Bobbie broke into the crowd. "Say, what's going on here? The young man outside said someone got hurt."

Dante looked up at the large man in a uniform of the London Metropolitan Police. "My wife has been injured. I need to get her to hospital. The young man just offered to summon a hackney."

The man nodded. "Lucky for you an ambulance was just returning to hospital after taking someone home." He looked around and extended his arms. "Everyone move back, please."

"Sweetheart, I'm going to have to shift you a tiny bit to lift you into my arms."

Lydia nodded and bit on her lip as he placed his other arm under her knees. This was the most dangerous part. If he shifted her so the knife penetrated her lung she would be dead before they reached the ambulance.

"Wait!" The young lad raced up. "The ambulance driver is bringing a stretcher."

Thank you, Lord. Lydia was growing weaker by the second. "I appreciate your help, young man."

"Dante," she whispered and took his hand. "I don't want to die."

He gritted his teeth, his stomach in knots. "You will not die. Do not even think that. The men with a stretcher are almost here. Soon you will be in hospital, and all will be well. I promise you." He knew his words were abrupt and curt, but he was hanging onto his own sanity by a thin thread.

CALLIE HUTTON

Not necessarily a praying man, Dante prayed with all his heart for his wife to survive and for forgiveness for promising her she would not die. He had very little experience with knife wounds, but this one didn't look good. He pushed those thoughts from his mind, or he would howl like a broken animal.

"Move back, please," the Bobbie said again. "Make room."

Slowly the gathering shuffled back, still gaping with morbid curiosity. Two men laid the stretcher on the ground next to Lydia.

"You will have to place her face first. She has an injury on her back." Dante hated releasing her, feeling as though as long as he held her he could keep her from dying.

The men nodded and with more gentleness than what he'd expected they moved her and placed her on the stretcher. A few gasps came from the crowd at the sight of the large knife sticking out of her back. Dante placed his hands on the floor, fighting the dizziness that tried to overtake him at the sight.

"Easy, lass, we'll have you in hospital in no time." One of the burly men holding the stretcher was a large Scot with long red flowing hair. He threw a blanket over her and then the two men lifted the stretcher. With a soft groan from Lydia, Dante was fairly certain that she'd passed out, which was good.

He climbed into the ambulance with her and placed his finger on her neck. A slight pulse, but nevertheless, he felt it. During the short ride, which did seem to take forever, he had time to reflect. There was no doubt in his mind that this was attempted murder. Had they been standing together at the time, most likely the two of them would have been stabbed. Hopefully, Lyons had been able to catch the man and drag him to the police station for questioning. They could hardly call this an accident.

Lydia remained unconscious the entire ride and then when

she was carried into hospital. A doctor was summoned and quickly ordered Lydia to an operating room.

"What happened?" the doctor asked as he and Dante followed the stretcher down a long corridor. The man oozed confidence. He was middle aged with silver streaks in his black hair. Just his presence was calming.

Dante ran his fingers through his hair. "Since I assume you see the knife sticking out from her back, that much you know. I can't give you more information for security purposes, but I am quite certain my wife was stabbed by a man—probably hired by another man—who has already killed two people."

The doctor merely shook his head. "I don't know what this world is coming to."

Once they reached a set of double doors, the doctor turned to him. "I will leave you here. When I am finished, I will meet you in the waiting room back down this corridor on the right-hand side."

"Thank you." Dante leaned over and kissed Lydia on her forehead and with a fear so great, he felt as though he would drop to his knees, he left.

Feeling at odds with himself, he wandered the corridor to the room the doctor had mentioned. With a quick change of mind, he strode to the front desk that they passed on their way in. A young man sat there and looked up at his approach. "Yes, sir?"

"I would like to send a note to family members. How do I do that?"

"We have a runner who works for the hospital. If you use that desk over there," he gestured to a small wooden desk next to the far wall, "I will have it delivered."

"Thank you."

Dante sat at the desk and found a stack of paper, two pens and a filled ink well. He penned a quick missive to Hunt, Driscoll and Lydia's father, Lord Sterling. His notes were brief, but with the urgency he felt. He hadn't wanted to trouble the doctor to give him any sort of prognosis since he'd rather have him working on Lydia, but the unknown was killing him.

He paced the corridor, the front room, and the street outside. About every five minutes he checked the waiting room where he was to meet the doctor.

All that time his head was spinning. One look at Lydia lying on the ground, pale-faced and looking as if she were already dead had hit him in the gut like a cannonball.

He could not live without her. Oh, he would wake each day and do his work, but never again would he feel the joy and love, yes love, that he felt for his wife. The sun would never shine again, and he would go through each day simply waiting to die.

What a fool he'd been thinking that leaping from one woman's bed to another's was a fulfilling life. He'd watched his two brothers succumb to their desire for their wives turn into love and laughed at them. Never would that happen to him, he assured his arrogant self.

Even when he married Lydia he didn't feel as though his heart was engaged. He liked her company, certainly desired her body, and thought if there were children, she would be a fine mother. But love?

No. That wasn't part of it.

He folded his hands and tapped his lips with his index fingers and stared at the floor as he paced and thought of the time they'd had together. He smiled at the contention when they'd first met and how he thought her an upright, overly-moral spinster with her head in books. She, in turn, thought him an arrogant rake with no morals and very little to recommend himself.

They were both wrong. Perhaps they brought the best out in each other. His head jerked up as Hunt and Diana came racing through the hospital door. "How is she? Your note didn't say much." Diana sat on a hard wooden chair in the front room and attempted to catch her breath.

Dante shrugged. "I haven't seen her or talked to the doctor since we brought her in." He waved to the waiting room. "Why don't we sit in there? That is where the doctor said he would meet me when the procedure was over."

They had barely settled when Driscoll and Amelia joined them, with Lord Sterling on their heels. The poor man looked dreadful. He was as pale as Lydia had been and looked as though he'd aged ten years. "How is my daughter? What happened?"

There was simply no way to answer in a kind way. "She was stabbed in the back at Paddington Station while I was buying our tickets. We had been working on that Home Office assignment, which is now finished, and were warned that we might be in danger. We were on our way to Bath to consult with a friend who might be able to help us when Lydia was attacked." He ran his fingers through his hair again. "We had a footman with us, but the culprit took advantage of the crowded station."

Dante hopped up and began to pace, slamming his fist into his palm. "I should have taken a carriage instead of the train. Or I should have left Lydia here under protection. I should have—"

Hunt stood and stepped in front of his brother. "Stop this, Dante. Two people were killed while being fully guarded. Let's just make sure Lydia is all right, and then, like it or not, the two of you need to be shipped off to the country until this is straightened out."

Everyone was assuming Lydia would be all right. But none of them had seen the knife. The huge knife sticking out of his wife's slender back. He felt as though he wanted to slam his fist into the wall.

"Mr. Rose." Dante turned to see the doctor standing in the doorway. He was covered in blood. Lydia's blood. Black dots appeared in Dante's eyes and he thought for a moment he would disgrace himself and pass out like some swooning debutante.

"Yes." He cleared his throat. "Yes. How is she doctor?"

The second it took the doctor to answer terrified him. Was she dead? *Oh God, no. Please don't take her from me. I will be the best husband in all of England. I will tell her how much I love her dozens of times a day.*

"It was a terrible wound," the doctor began. "Fortunately for her the knife missed her lung and her heart. That would probably have taken her life. Upon examination it appeared no main arteries were involved. We cleaned her up, stitched the wound closed and I am confident the young lady will survive."

Dante covered his face with his hands, then turned on his heels and left the room. He barreled through the front door of the hospital and charged down the street, going nowhere, tears sliding down his cheeks. She would not die. He would have her for years. And years, and years.

Forever.

* * *

"DANTE, for heaven's sake. I'm fine. Stop coddling me." Lydia grew grouchier by the day and she felt bad about that. But the man she married, the arrogant, devil-may-care rake had become a hovering nanny.

It had been three weeks since she'd been stabbed at Paddington Station. She understood from Hunt and Driscoll that Dante had been almost crazed with panic that she would die. But he refused to leave her alone since she arrived back from hospital.

Even while under guards that he had hired while she was there hadn't assuaged his fear. Once dismissed from hospital, he'd kept her in their bedchamber at Hunt's townhouse while he scoured London looking for the man who had stabbed her. Lyons had done his best, but the man managed to escape in the crowd the day she'd been stabbed.

"I'm not coddling you," he said in answer to her complaint. "I just want you to take it easy for a while."

She sighed. "It's been three weeks. I can certainly take a stroll outside."

He opened his mouth, most likely to once again tell her nothing was safe when a knock on the door drew their attention.

Hunt entered at their permission, a cream-colored envelope in his hand. "This just came by special delivery for you." He handed it to Dante.

"Thank you." He slid the paper out of the envelope and looked over at Lydia, who sat on the settee in the chamber, her arms crossed, scowling at him. His eyes moved back and forth as he read the missive. He folded the paper and placed it on the table in front of her. "It's over."

She uncrossed her arms and sat forward, wincing slightly at the remaining pain in her back. "What?"

Hunt sauntered over and sat next to her, taking her hand in his.

"Was that from the Home Office?"

"Yes." Dante leaned back and rested his foot on his knee. "They apparently were able to connect the Ambassador to the murders of his contact and her lover, as well as your attempted murder."

Lydia's jaw dropped. "He *was* the one behind it? But I thought he'd been granted immunity because of his status. Why would he want to see us dead?"

"Dear old boy Mr. Ambassador, was also working with the Russians. He was being investigated by the German government for that. When I visited with Sir Phillip while you were recovering, he gave me that information. It was for that reason the Ambassador had not been called back to Germany. They were doing their own investigation and planned to use us and the other two as witnesses against him. Especially with your knowledge of Russian."

Lydia shook her head. "This is quite complicated. I remember the woman he received the information from spoke to him in Russian. It never occurred to me he was selling information from England to Russia, and not his own country."

"He was probably doing both. A very special sort of traitor."

The three sat in silence processing the information. Finally, Dante stood and walked to the fireplace behind the settee and leaned his arm on the mantel. "That note," he gestured with his head at the envelope still sitting on the table, "was to advise us that the Ambassador committed suicide yesterday."

Lydia sucked in a deep breath. "Oh, no. That's terrible."

Dante looked over at her and smiled. "Sweetheart, the man tried to have you killed."

"Yes. That is true." She stood and moved over to Dante, wrapping her arms around his waist and leaning onto his strong, warm chest. "I'm just so glad it's over."

He rested his chin on her head. "Me too, sweetheart, me too."

Hunt slapped his thighs and stood. "I'm glad it's all finished. I'm sure you don't need me anymore." With a chuckle he left the room.

Dante leaned back and looked at her. "Don't ever do that to me again."

"Do what?"

"Almost get yourself killed."

Lydia laughed at how serious he looked. "Dante, I had no intention of getting myself killed, and do not plan to do the same ever again."

"I don't think I've said it enough, but I love you, Lydia. I don't want anything to happen to you."

Her heart lifted. He'd told her so many times since the stabbing that he loved her, couldn't live without her, and he had been a complete fool and idiot to think love would never come his way.

She stared up at him. "And I love you, too, Dante."

"Say it again."

"I love you too, Dante."

He leaned down and covered her mouth with his. Lydia sighed against his lips. Yes, there was such a thing as a happy ending. Even for an intellectual and a rake.

Did you like this story? Please consider leaving a review on either Goodreads or the place where you bought it. Long or short, your review will help other readers discover new authors and make purchasing decisions!

I hope you had fun reading Lydia and Dante's love story. *An Inconvenient Arrangement* is the third book in the Rose Room Rogues series.

Look for *A Rose for Laura*, book 4 in the Rose Room Rogue series.

Keniel Rose, a bi-racial bastard son of the former Earl of Huntington is unknown to his three brothers. He was born to Chloe Singh, an artist mother who was half Jamaican and half Indian. She had an affair with the former Earl of Huntington when he was there to check on one of his plantations.

On her deathbed she tells Keniel of his heritage and encourages him to find his family. He sets out for London and is soon employed at The Rose Room, while his brothers, the owners, do not know who he is.

Miss Laura Benson is an almost spinster who champions children on the London streets. She's raised enough money to rent a house for an orphanage. She is upset to learn that a Mr. Keniel Singh has put in a bid to buy the house for himself. She visits him and finds a young, handsome, charming man who won't give up the purchase of 'her' house.

Keniel is attracted to the spirited, beautiful woman, but holds back, sure she would never consider any sort of relationship with him because of his heritage. However, to keep her in his life, he refuses to break the contract for the house. Instead, he offers to help her find another one.

Laura is equally attracted to the man, but his refusal to allow her the house that she deems perfect for the children, and the fact that he manages a gambling house patronized by the very men who produce these cast off children warns her to keep her heart close.

Let the battles begin.

Visit my website for more information:
https://calliehutton.com/book/a-rose-for-laura/

You can find a list of all my books on my website:
http://calliehutton.com/books/

ABOUT THE AUTHOR

**Receive a free book and stay up to date with new releases
and sales!
http://calliehutton.com/newsletter/**

USA Today bestselling author, Callie Hutton, has penned more
than 45 historical romance and cozy mystery books. She lives
in Oklahoma with her very close and lively family, which
includes her twin grandsons, affectionately known as "The
Twinadoes."

Callie loves to hear from readers. Contact her directly at cal-
liehutton11@gmail.com or find her online at www.calliehut-
ton.com.

Connect with her on Facebook, Twitter, and Goodreads.

Follow her on BookBub to receive notice of new releases, preorders, and special promotions.

Praise for books by Callie Hutton

A Study in Murder

"This book is a delight!...*A Study in Murder* has clear echoes of Jane Austen, Agatha Christie, and of course, Sherlock Holmes. You will love this book." —William Bernhardt, author of *The Last Chance Lawyer*

"A one-of-a-kind new series that's packed with surprises." —Mary Ellen Hughes, National bestselling author of *A Curio Killing*.

"[A] lively and entertaining mystery...I predict a long run for this smart series." —Victoria Abbott, award-winning author of The Book Collector Mysteries

"With a breezy style and alluring, low-keyed humor, Hutton crafts a charming mystery with a delightful, irrepressible sleuth." —Madeline Hunter, *New York Times* bestselling author of *Never Deny a Duke*

The Elusive Wife

"I loved this book and you will too. Jason is a hottie & Oliva is the kind of woman we'd all want as a friend. Read it!" —Cocktails and Books

"In my experience I've had a few hits but more misses with historical romance so I was really pleasantly surprised to be

hooked from the start by obviously good writing." —Book
Chick City

"The historic elements and sensory details of each scene make
the story come to life, and certainly helps immerse the reader
in the world that Olivia and Jason share." —The Romance
Reviews

"You will not want to miss *The Elusive Wife*." —My Book
Addiction

"...it was a well written plot and the characters were likeable."
—Night Owl Reviews

A Run for Love

"An exciting, heart-warming Western love story!" —*New York
Times* bestselling author Georgina Gentry

"I loved this book!!! I read the BEST historical romance last
night...It's called *A Run For Love*." —*New York Times* bestselling
author Sharon Sala

"This is my first Callie Hutton story, but it certainly won't be
my last." —The Romance Reviews

An Angel in the Mail

"...a warm fuzzy sensuous read. I didn't put it down until I was
done." —Sizzling Hot Reviews

Visit www.calliehutton.com for more information.

Made in the USA
Las Vegas, NV
04 July 2021